You're Nobody 'Til Somebody Kills You

Also by Robert J. Randisi

You're Nobody 'Til Somebody Kills You

ROBERT J. RANDISI

Minotaur Books

A THOMAS DUNNE BOOK

NEW YORK

A THOMAS DUNNE BOOK FOR MINOTAUR BOOKS.
An imprint of St. Martin's Publishing Group.

YOU'RE NOBODY 'TIL SOMEBODY KILLS YOU. Copyright © 2009 by Robert J. Randisi. All rights reserved. Printed in the United States of America. For information, address St. Martin's Press, 175 Fifth Avenue, New York, N.Y. 10010.

www.thomasdunnebooks.com
www.minotaurbooks.com

Library of Congress Cataloging-in-Publication Data

Randisi, Robert J.
    You're nobody 'til somebody kills you / Robert J. Randisi. — 1st ed.
        p. cm. — (A Rat Pack mystery)
    "A Thomas Dunne book for Minotaur Books" —T.p. verso.
    ISBN 978-0-312-37643-7
    1. Rat Pack (Entertainers)—Fiction. 2. Monroe, Marilyn, 1926-1962—Fiction. I. Title.
    PS3568.A53Y68 2009
    813'.54—dc22

                                                     2009012737

First Edition: September 2009

10 9 8 7 6 5 4 3 2 1

This is for Marthayn. The actual song title is "You're Nobody 'Til Somebody LOVES You," and when I met you I found out that was very true.

You're Nobody 'Til Somebody Kills You

Prologue

Las Vegas, Nevada
Spring 2003

I LIKE THE FLAMINGO, and the Riv. Along with the Golden Nugget, Binions and a few other places, they're the last vestiges of my Las Vegas—the Las Vegas of Frank and Dean and Sammy. Now it's the Vegas of Howie Mandel, Siegfried and Roy and Danny Gans—talented, yes. The Rat Pack? Hardly.

I had a meeting at the Riviera that day. Some kid journalist wanted an interview about the old days, and when anybody wanted to talk about the old days they came to Eddie G.

"Hey, Eddie," a blackjack dealer shouted as I walked by, "how the hell are ya, man?"

"Good, good." I didn't know his name, but I knew the face. It made an old man feel good when the youngsters working Vegas recognized me.

I went past the bar, and it's, "Hey, Eddie, have a drink, man." Past the pit and they said, "Mr. Gianelli," respectfully, because I made the pit what it is today. And when a waitress stopped to kiss my cheek, let me smell her perfume and breathed, "Hey, Eddie," into my ear—well, I ain't dead, ya know. I popped wood—or what passes for wood when you're eighty-two.

Just like me the hip life has passed the Riviera by, but I still liked it. I told the journalist to meet me in Kady's coffee shop at 8:00 A.M. Me, I don't sleep so much, anymore. I'm usually up around five or six, and Kady's is a twenty-four-hour joint.

I stopped in the doorway, looked around. There were a few customers. Some had just gotten up, others hadn't been to bed yet. But they all had the same look in their eyes. Tired.

Except for one. A young girl who seemed wide-awake and eager. I was looking for a writer named J.T. Kerouac. A friend of mine had set it up, but if the writer was a girl he would've mentioned it. Unless he figured it would be funny.

The girl jumped up out of her booth when she saw me and hurried over.

"Mr. Gianelli?" she asked, all excited.

"Eddie G," I said. "Everybody calls me Eddie G."

"Eddie, I'm so happy to meet you," she said. "I'm J.T. Kerouac. No relation."

"I knew Jack," I said. "Well, I met him. I wouldn't say I knew him."

"Wow," she gushed. "See, that's why I wanted to interview you. You're a legend in Vegas. They say that Eddie G knew everybody."

"How old are you, Kerouac?"

"Twenty-four," she said, with a grin. "I know, I look younger. It's the freckles—but they go with my red hair. Nothing I can do about it. I really am a writer, though. Want to see my ID?"

I hesitated, then said, "Okay, Kerouac. Let's have some coffee."

We walked to her booth. The table was covered with papers and a lined pad. There was also a laptop computer, and books—about half a dozen, some hardback, some paper—all having to do with the Rat Pack, with Frank and Dean, and one on Marilyn Monroe.

She sat down and I slid across from her.

The waitress came over and said, "Hi, Eddie. It's good ta see you. How ya doin'?"

"Good, Melina, real good."

"This gonna be separate checks?"

"No," I said, "I'll take care of it—"

"No, no, I invited you," J.T. said. "It's on me."

"I'll start with coffee, Melina."

"Sure thing, Eddie.

"I'm sensing a theme," I said, gesturing toward the books.

"Oh, these? I'm working on a documentary. I'm a writer, and a filmmaker. When I'm making a film I'm also the director and the producer."

"Not the camera . . . woman?"

"I have a cameraman, actually," she said, "and a soundman."

"And what's the documentary about?"

"The Rat Pack, and their women. And I don't only mean their girlfriends and wives. I mean women who were fringe Rat Packers . . . sort of . . ."

"And what am I here to be interviewed about?"

"Old Las Vegas," she said. "Vegas has been turned into a huge theme park."

"Tell me about it."

"I'm going to write about the way it used to be, and nobody knows more about that than you."

"And that's what you need me for today?"

"No, today I'm working on a piece for *Las Vegas Magazine*."

"And who are you making the documentary for?"

"Well . . . for me. I'm hoping to place it with one of the cable stations—HBO, maybe A&E, or even Bravo."

"How's it going?"

She had been typing on the laptop while talking. Now she stopped, sat back and looked at me.

"Actually, it's not going very well."

"Why not?"

She touched the book on Marilyn. I saw the name Spoto on the spine.

"Everything I've found on Marilyn seems to be old news," she said. "I have some stuff on Angie Dickinson, and Shirley MacLaine, even Ruta Lee."

"There should be more on Marilyn Monroe than on those women combined," I said.

"Oh, there is," she said, "but it's all been done before. Over and over. I need something new, and I just can't find it."

I drummed my fingers on the table. Even Eddie G wants to impress a pretty young girl. It had been awhile since somebody like J.T. had looked at me with such admiration.

"What?" she asked. "What's going on, Mr. Gianelli?"

"Eddie," I said, "call me Eddie."

"What's on your mind, Eddie?"

"Old Vegas," I said, "and Marilyn."

"Did you know Marilyn, Eddie?" she asked, leaning forward.

"Yep."

"Well?"

"Well enough."

"Don't play games, Eddie," she said. "This documentary is important to me. If you can help me—"

"Breakfast," I said.

"What?"

"I need some more coffee, and some breakfast," I told her.

She worried her pretty lower lip, then said, "And then what?"

"And then I have a story to tell," I said, "about old Las Vegas, and Marilyn . . ."

One

DEAN MARTIN SAID, "Twenty-two, pay the lady!"

The crowd erupted into applause as Dino paid off the beautiful brunette, who probably wasn't even legally old enough to gamble. That's not my department, though. Once they're in, they're in.

Only Dino could get away with paying a gambler when they actually busted the hand. Immediately afterward he spread his hands and backed away, giving the regular dealer back his table. Then he walked over to me with a big grin on his handsome face.

"Eddie, my man! I came lookin' for you."

We shook hands warmly.

"Been a few months," I said.

"Well, I'm back," he said. "Actually, we're back. Three of us, anyway."

I knew that Frank, Dean and Sammy were booked into the Sands for one night, on the twenty-third. I had expected a call from one of them, but didn't think Dean would come looking for me in my pit.

we can have a drink?"

nk, Dean or Sammy I could pretty much
I wanted to. My boss, Jack Entratter,
they wanted—like the power to pay

...a get somebody to fill in," I said. "How about we
in the Silver Queen in ten minutes?"

Dean's smile broadened. "I'll be waitin', pally."

I got to the Silver Queen lounge in eight minutes. Dean was sitting
at the bar talking to the bartender. Folks seated at the tables were
pointing at him and talking excitedly to each other, but no one
approached him. At the moment there was no one performing.

I approached the bar and Dean turned, gave me that famous
smile again. He had a cigarette in one hand, and a partially finished drink in the other. Dean always had a drink and a cigarette
on stage, but I knew the whole drink thing was a put-up job for
the "Clydes" in the audience. In fact, I'd been on the set of *Ser-
geants 3* the previous summer to shoot a couple of scenes the guys
had cast me in for fun, and I never saw Dean drunk the whole
time. Ruta Lee, the leading lady of the film, had been quoted saying the same thing. She also complained that the guys treated her
like a little sister. Well, everybody but me. Ruta Lee was quite a
dish.

But Dean's smoking, that was for real. In fact, Dean, Frank
and Sammy—who all made their living with their voices—were
heavy smokers.

"Bourbon, Eddie?"

"You know it." Now *my* drinking, that was for real, too.

He turned to the bartender, Lew, who nodded and gave me a
wave. I took the seat next to Dean.

"Kind of odd for you to come in this early for a one-night
show," I said.

"I know," he said. "Frank and Sammy will be in tomorrow. They want you to have dinner with us."

"Be my pleasure." Lew set my drink down. "I saw Sammy here a couple of months ago, and Joey last month. I haven't seen Frank since Tahoe."

"I remember," he said. "Seems like we always come to you when we're in trouble, Eddie."

"What are friends for?"

"Well," he said, "we should be your friends even when we're not in trouble."

"I'm invited to dinner tomorrow night, right?" I asked. "I don't guess that's because all three of you are in trouble."

"No, it's because all three of us like you, Eddie," Dean said, "and we wouldn't come to Vegas without seein' you."

"I appreciate that, Dean," I said. "And I understand it." I sipped my drink. "So, tomorrow that's just for pleasure. Right?"

"Right."

"And tonight's for . . ."

"You're a smart man, Eddie."

"Sometimes I think so, too," I said.

"It isn't one of us who has a problem this time," Dean said. "It's a friend."

"A good friend?"

"Yes."

"A . . . girl?"

"It's not what you think," Dean said. "I've known this lady for a long time. She's kind of . . . delicate. When she came to me with her problem I knew you were the man to help her. You know how to keep a low profile."

"Yeah," I said, "that's something you guys aren't so good at."

Dean smiled.

"Never been high on any of our lists, I guess."

"Okay," I said, "so when do I meet the lady?"

"How's tomorrow sound?" he asked. "We can take a ride to Tahoe in the morning."

"Tahoe? Why there?"

"Vegas makes her nervous. She's staying at the Cal Neva as Frank's guest."

"Is this somebody equally as high-profile as you guys?"

Dean raised his glass and asked, "Why ruin the surprise, pally?"

Two

I WAS BACK in my pit ten minutes when Jack Entratter approached.

"Jack," I said, as he reached me, "what are you doing around so late?"

"What's late?" he said, shrugging his shoulders, adjusting his jacket. "I'm here all the time, Eddie, you know that."

He was, and he wasn't. Jack was around whenever he wanted to be. He had a house, but he also had a room in the hotel. In fact, his mother had a room, too.

But he was on the floor, and at my pit, and it was almost midnight. This was not normal.

"Listen," he said, "Frank, Dean and Sammy will be here tomorrow. They want you to have dinner with them tomorrow night. That ain't a problem, is it?"

"No, Jack," I said, "that's not a problem."

"Good," he said, "good, Eddie." He patted me on the shoulder. Now, that was unusual.

"Anything else, Jack?"

Jack hesitated. Something was on his mind, but he wasn't sure he wanted to bring it up.

"Well . . . my nephew's comin' to town," he said. "Richard. You've never met him."

"No, I haven't." I hadn't even known Jack had a nephew.

"Yeah, well . . . you'll get your chance. I want to show the kid a good time."

"What's the kid's game? Or do you want a girl—"

"No, no," Jack said, "nothin' like that, Eddie. He's a good kid. Not old enough to gamble, and my sister would kill me if I fixed him up . . . you know."

"Oh, I get it, Jack."

"Yeah." He looked around, shrugged his shoulders again. "I ain't really that sure how to entertain him, ya know?"

"There's a lot to do in Vegas, Jack," I said. "I'll get him a ticket for the show."

"That'll be good," he said. "My sister, she loves Frank."

I didn't want to say that his nephew might like somebody like Paul Anka, or Fabian, better.

"Uh, Jack, I'm going to need the chopper tomorrow morning, and some time off."

"Time off? For what?"

"Dean wants to go to Tahoe."

"You saw Dino?"

"Tonight," I said. "He dealt some blackjack, and then we had a drink."

"He's here early," Jack said.

"Yeah."

"Well . . . his suite's always waitin' for him."

"I know that."

"What's he want to go to Tahoe for?"

"I'm not really sure."

"Okay," he said, scratching his cheek, "okay, yeah, sure, take 'im to Tahoe. Let him do what he wants to do."

"Sure, Jack."

Jack looked around, didn't seem like he wanted to walk away.

"Hey, boss, what's goin' on?"

"Hmm?"

"You're . . . distracted."

"Yeah, well," he said, "I've been talkin' to my sister, and my mother . . . Richard gets in tomorrow morning. I gotta pick him up at the airport . . ."

"Did you want me to pick him up?" I asked. "Was that what you were gonna ask me?"

"Naw, naw, Eddie," he said, "I wouldn't ask ya to do that. You ain't a chauffeur. Besides, my sister and my mother would both have my ass if I didn't pick him up myself."

"Well, I wouldn't want to get them mad at me."

"No, believe me," he said, "you wouldn't. I'm gonna take a walk around the place, Eddie. When do you get off?"

"Three."

"I'll see you tomorrow then—stop in whenever you get back from Tahoe. I'd like to know what's goin' on."

"Sure, Jack."

"See ya, Eddie."

"Later, boss."

I watched him as he wandered around the room. He stopped and spoke to some of the players, didn't talk to any of the other employees he came across, except for a pretty waitress. Jack liked to keep the Sands stocked with waitresses, hatcheck girls and cigarette girls who looked like they belonged on stage.

Once Jack left the casino floor I relaxed a bit and was able to go back to work. Kind of. I guess I was also wondering what Dean wanted to show me in Tahoe.

Or who.

Three

DEAN HAD MADE the arrangements for a car to pick us up early the next morning and take us to the airfield. The chopper pilot was the same one who had flown me to Reno and Tahoe several times the previous year when I was trying, at Frank's request, to help Sammy out of a jam. I had been successful, and had not seen the pilot since then.

He greeted us in a friendly manner, as if he had known us both a long time, calling us "gents," and showing no surprise or awe that one of his passengers was Dean Martin.

In the chopper Dean told me that Frank had almost finished his refurbishment of the Cal Neva, but would not be there when we arrived.

"He's flying into Vegas later today from Palm Springs. He's still getting the guesthouse ready for JFK to stay there in March."

"Is that gonna happen?" I asked Dean.

"Between you and me," Dean said, "I wouldn't hold my breath. JFK's people are not gonna stand for it. Frank's in for a big surprise."

"Have you tried to tell him?"

"Once," Dean said. "He insists that he and Jack are friends. He's gonna have to find out for himself—and I hope I'm not around when he does. He's even putting in a helipad."

"Man, that's gotta be expensive."

"The whole project is costing Frank a fortune."

At that point we were both tired of shouting over the noise of the rotating blades so we put our conversation on hold until we were on the ground.

There was a car waiting to take us to the Cal Neva. It sure didn't look to me like the work was almost done, but then what did I know about construction? The cabins in the back were still there. One was Frank's, one was for his buddies when they came to town—that was the one I'd stayed in last year—and the other was for Frank's, uh, lady friends. Years later the press would label Shirley MacLaine, Angie Dickinson and Ruta Lee Lady Rat Packers. I was always careful not to say Rat Pack around Frank. He didn't like the name. He always referred to him and his buddies as "the Clan," and their shows at the Sands as "the Summit." It was the newspapers that dubbed them the "Rat Pack."

Anyway, I assumed—when the car pulled to a stop in front of cabin number three—that one of Frank and Dino's lady pals needed help. I was kind of hoping it would be Angie Dickinson, but for selfish reasons. I had always had a thing for her, and meeting her had only strengthened the feeling.

"Here we are," Dean said.

I looked at him.

"You comin'?"

"No," Dean said. "I told her you were gonna talk to her."

"Alone?"

"Yep."

I looked up at the front of the cabin. When I walked through that door I'd be alone with whoever was inside. Suddenly, I was as nervous as a schoolboy that it might be Angie.

"Dean?"

"Yeah?"

"It's not Angie, is it?"

"Angie Dickinson? Hell, no. Why would you think that? There ain't nothin' fragile about Angie. That broad is a rock."

"And this one's not, huh?"

"No, Eddie," Dean said, "this one's not. You'll have to take it easy with her. Listen to her, talk to her, but tread lightly, my friend."

"What makes you think she'll trust me?"

"The two of you have met," Dean said.

"When?"

"She was very impressed."

"Come on, Dean," I said, "who's in there?"

"You'll see."

"What makes her so fragile?"

"You'll find out for yourself," he said.

"Why so secretive?"

"Well," Dean said with a bemused expression, "if I told you who was inside, maybe you wouldn't get out of the car."

"Now I'm really curious."

He smiled and said, "I'll wait here."

I got out of the car, went up the steps to the door and stopped. I looked down at the car, but couldn't see if Dean was laughing at me or not. I knocked. When the door opened I caught my breath.

Four

BLOND HAIR, RED MOUTH, flawless, pale skin. To the public at
large that's what Marilyn Monroe was. But they had never seen
the Marilyn who was standing in front of me at that moment.

"Eddie," she said, in that breathy voice of hers. "Come on
in."

I entered the cottage, speechless, and closed the door behind
me. She was wearing a pair of capri pants that hugged her as-
sets, and a sweater that listed to one side, leaving a single shoulder bare. A single smooth, creamy shoulder, I might add.

"Miss Monroe—" I started, but she turned quickly, her hair
swinging into her eyes. She tossed it back with a quick jerk.

"Please, Eddie," she said, "call me Marilyn. Is Dean outside?"

"Yeah—yes, he said you wanted to see me alone. Marilyn, I
don't understand. We've only met once, and that was for about
three minutes."

She laughed, her beautiful face brightening at the memory of
that moment. "I remember very well. It was last year in Harrah's
in Reno. You rescued me from a crowd of people and helped me
get to the elevator."

"And that was it," I said. "We haven't seen each other or spoken since then."

"Oh, but Eddie," she said, "I have to tell you, the way you took control? I don't think I've ever felt safer. And I feel safe with you now."

"Well, I wasn't all that smart that time," I said. "I was so involved in what I was doing I thought you were in town shooting *The Misfits* with Gable."

"B-but . . . Clark died months before that, like twelve days after we finished shooting."

"Sure, I knew that. I felt real stupid later when I thought back on it."

"I was in town doing some publicity."

Suddenly, her eyes got sad—the way they'd been when she opened the door—and her mouth quivered. And it wasn't the famous Marilyn mouth I was looking at.

"Eddie—" she said, reaching a hand out to me blindly as tears filled her eyes.

"Hey, hey," I said, taking her hand and leading her to a chair. She sat down and I crouched down in front of her.

Marilyn couldn't help herself. Even in that moment she was radiating not only sex, but sadness. I knew what Dean had meant when he said I'd see for myself how fragile she was. Of course I'd heard stories of her moods. Also, her tumultuous love life, marriage and divorce from famous men like Joe DiMaggio and playwright Arthur Miller, a love affair with Frank that ended when he got engaged to Juliet Prowse.

Right at that moment, though, Marilyn looked alone and bewildered—much the way she had looked that day in Harrah's Casino in Reno. The crowd had surrounded her and she had no one with her to help. I'd stepped in, took her to the elevator, and barely had time to tell her my name before the doors closed. But she'd had time to say, "Thank you, Eddie." Later, after I finished with Sammy's business and things were back to normal I'd think

about that moment, play back in my head Marilyn Monroe saying my name.

Now I was alone in a room with her—not with the screen
star, the icon, every boy or man's wet dream—I was in a room
with the real Marilyn—sad, lonely Norma Jean who, I sensed,
was also very afraid of something.

"It's okay, Marilyn," I said. I pulled another chair over, sat
next to her and took both her hands in mine.

"Dean said you could help me, Eddie."

"And I will, Marilyn," I said. How could I not? "But for me
to do that, you have to tell me what's wrong."

"Oh, Eddie," she said, squeezing my hands, "when it comes
to my life, the question is . . . what's right?"

Five

"Eddie," MARILYN SAID, in that little girl voice, "I'm being watched—followed."

I stared at her. Dean had said she was fragile, he didn't say anything about her being paranoid. And I have to admit, I never read gossip—well, except for Hedda and Louella, and that was really only after I had met Frank, Dean, Sammy and Joey. It was kind of my way of checking up on them.

The only TV I watched was detective and Western shows and—again—when the guys appeared on their own show, or someone else's.

My point is, if Marilyn had a reputation for paranoia I hadn't heard about it. But so far everything Dean had told me I'd see, I had, so I had to believe my eyes, and ears.

If she said she was being watched, and followed, I had to take it seriously.

"By who?" I asked.

"I—I don't know."

"Okay, then why?"

"I don't know that, either." She shrugged, and her sweater

fell lower down one shoulder. I was just glad she wasn't wearing any of the stuff she'd worn in *Some Like It Hot*—that white, sparkly dress, the loose-fitting sweater she kept falling out of? That was, in fact, the hottest I'd ever seen her look, and I was having a hard enough time concentrating.

"I have an idea, though . . ." she said.

"Marilyn, tell me whatever you can."

"Well . . . after Clark died the newspapers were saying it was shooting *The Misfits* that killed him."

"Was it a tough shoot?" The film had been out almost a year, but I hadn't seen it yet.

"Very tough. He insisted on doing his own stunts, even though he was sick."

"Did everyone on the movie know he was sick?"

"No," she said, "he kept it to himself. Even John Huston, the director, didn't know."

"So?"

"He suffered two heart attacks, and the second one killed him," she said. Then she released my hands and covered her face. "They said it was all the stress on the set that killed him . . . that because I made him wait and wait . . . that I was responsible."

Jesus, I thought, what a thing for her to have to live with.

I crouched in front of her again, took her in my arms to soothe her. There I was with everybody's sex symbol and I felt like I was holding a child. If someone had told me even yesterday that I could hold Marilyn Monroe in my arms and not be aroused I'd have called them a liar. But all I could think was, this poor kid . . .

"Marilyn, come on . . . you just told me how hard a shoot it was."

"Yes," she said, "but the newspapers didn't talk about that, didn't talk about what John Huston had put him through . . . didn't mention that he smoked three packs a day . . . or that he'd lost forty pounds in a hurry to do the movie. No, it was all about me. . . ."

"But you know that wasn't true."

"But it was," she said, sitting back and dropping her hands. Tears made her face glisten, her eyes were wide with . . . with what? Fright? "He was like a father to me on that film, Eddie, and yet I made him wait and wait for me to get to the set . . . do you think I was trying to punish my father?"

Well, now it was clear that Marilyn had been under *some* sort of analysis, because a shrink had to have put that thought in her head.

"I don't believe that for a minute."

She made an *O* with her beautiful mouth and then said, "You don't?"

Okay, *now* I was excited.

I got back into my chair and crossed my legs.

"Marilyn, do you think maybe it's reporters following you?"

"It could be," she said, "but they come right at me with flashbulbs going off. Oh, some of them hide behind trees, try to catch me sun bathing in the nude, or swimming, you know . . . but this is different." She looked horrified then and added, "This is . . . *sinister*!"

I studied her face for a few moments, no hardship while I did some quick thinking. What was it Dean thought I could do for her? See if she was being tailed?

"Are you planning to stop in Reno, or Vegas?" I asked.

"No," she said, "I have no reason to go to Reno, and I—I don't like Vegas. Frank just said I could stay here for a while, to . . . to get away."

"And do you think you were followed here?"

She looked down.

"I don't want you to think I'm crazy, Eddie."

"I don't think that, Marilyn."

"I felt there was someone on the plane with me, and then at

the airport. Since I got here two days ago I haven't gone out . . .
I haven't even gone near the windows, so . . . I don't know if
anyone is . . . out there."

I resisted the urge to go and look out the window.

"How much longer will you be here?" I asked.

"A couple of days," she said. "I—I have to get back, I'm buy-
ing a house."

"Well, that's good, right?"

She didn't answer, but rushed across the room and came
back with a script, which she handed me.

"And I'm reading this," she said. "I'm supposed to make it
with Dean, and Cyd Charisse."

Yikes, I thought, Cyd Charisse and Marilyn in the same
movie? Where's a guy supposed to look? I checked out the title
page: *Something's Got to Give.* It had screenplay by Arnold
Shulman and Nunnally Johnson printed on it.

"It's being rewritten again, but it's a remake of the Cary
Grant and Irene Dunne film *My Favorite Wife.*"

I vaguely recalled the film. I've never understood the neces-
sity of remakes. Wasn't there enough new stuff out there waiting
to be made?

"Anyway," she said, taking the script back, "I didn't want to
do it, but I owe the studio a picture, and I'll get to work with
George again."

I found out later that "George" was George Cukor, with whom
she'd worked once before. I also found out that she'd been talked
into doing the movie by the same people who talked her into buy-
ing a house alone. Marilyn could be talked into things.

She could probably also be talked out of things, like the idea
she was being watched. But first I had to make sure she wasn't.

"Eddie," she asked, after putting the script back where she'd
gotten it from, "can you help me?"

What could I say?

I stood up.

"Let me see what I can find out, Marilyn," I said. "Meanwhile, you relax here and read your script. Keep doing what you've been doing. Don't go out and don't go near the windows."

"Oh, Eddie," she gasped. She hugged me, laying her head against my chest. I put my arms around her. The scent of her filled my nostrils. I felt like a sinner and a saint at the same time. Millions of men would have willingly changed places with me at that moment.

"It'll be okay, kid," I said.

"I know," she said, squeezing me tightly. "I feel as safe with you as I did with Robert Mitchum in the Canadian Rockies when we were shooting *River of No Return*."

Huh, I thought, Robert Mitchum. I guess it could've been worse.

"You bastard," I said to Dean when I got back in the car.

"I told you," he said.

"You still could've warned me."

"I had to let you see for yourself," he said. "She's more than just a hot broad, isn't she? She's more than just Marilyn Monroe."

"Yeah," I said, "she's more—a helluva lot more. Now let's get back to Vegas. I've got some phone calls to make."

"My man, Eddie G!" Dean said happily. "You're gonna help her?"

"I'm gonna help her," I said, "but first I gotta take a cold shower."

Six

Back in Vegas, driving from McCarron Airport to the Sands, I asked Dean about his relationship with Marilyn.

"I met her before Joe DiMaggio, and before Frank did. It was back in '53, when I was still making films with Jerry. She was a sweet kid. She's still a sweet kid, Eddie, but there's something . . . broken about her. She's been taken advantage of . . . a lot! I'll really appreciate it if you can help her. Even if you just ease her mind some."

"What about this new picture she's supposed to make with you?" I asked. "*Something's Got to Give?*"

"Jesus, what a mess," he said, shaking his head. He lit a cigarette, let the smoke drift out his nose, then held the cigarette between the first two fingers of his right hand. "I'd love to make a film with Marilyn and Cyd, but this one's a mess. We're on our second producer and third writer. Everybody involved with this film feels trapped."

"Including you?"

"Hell, not me, pally," he said, picking a piece of tobacco from his tongue, "I don't even think it's gonna get made."

"Why not?"

"Because as soon as they try to replace Marilyn," he said, "I'm gonna walk."

When we reached the Sands, Dean went to see if the guys had checked in.

"You gonna rehearse?" I asked.

He laughed. "Pally, I'm gonna pretend you didn't ask that. And don't forget, we're havin' dinner tonight with Frank and Sammy. Nine sharp. Be out front, we'll pick you up in a limo."

In the lobby of the Sands we split up. I didn't have an office of my own, so whenever I needed to sit down and use a phone I'd go to Marcia Clarkson's office. Marcy—which was what her friends called her—made sure everybody at the Sands got paid.

As I entered her office, she pointed without looking and said, "Use that desk over there."

"What makes you think I need—"

She looked up at me and smiled. She was pretty, with frizzy hair and thick glasses. We'd dated a few times and, when she was dressed for the evening, she was downright beautiful. We never clicked romantically, but stayed friends—even after I introduced her to my buddy, Danny Bardini. He was a bigger player than I was and had the added cachet of being a private eye. *77 Sunset Strip*, *Peter Gunn* and *Hawaiian Eye* had made private eyes cool and romantic.

"Eddie, you never come to my office just to say hello, do you?"

"Well . . . no, but I'll start."

"Yeah, sure," she said, "right after today."

I stopped to kiss the top of her head and then went to the desk she'd offered. Dialing Danny Bardini's number, I reminded myself to keep my voice down. Even though she'd stayed friends with me, Marcy's opinion of Danny wasn't very high. That was because he'd slept with her before deciding to move on. I keep telling myself it pays to be a gentleman.

"Bardini Investigations," Penny O'Grady answered.

"You haven't quit on him yet?" I asked.

"Have you got a job for me at the Sands?"

"Of course."

"One where I don't have to wear fishnets?"

"Well . . ."

"What do you need, Eddie?"

"The man, if he's there."

"Hold on."

After a click Danny said, "Hey, buddy, what's shakin'?"

"I'm gonna tell you, Danny, but you've got to promise you won't go off the deep end."

"Uh-oh," he said, "one of your big stars in trouble again?"

"Maybe."

"And you need ol' Danny Boy to help clean it up," he said. "I'm there, ol' buddy. Which one we talkin' about? Frank? Dino?"

"Well, Dino asked me to help a friend of his."

"He's the coolest cat on earth," Danny said. "Count me in. Who's the pal?"

I hesitated. Did I really want Danny in on this? That was the question. The answer was, who else could I trust?

"Marilyn Monroe."

Silence on the other end.

"Danny?"

"I'm here," he said, "I'm just tryin' to think if I heard you right."

"You did."

"I get to meet her?"

"If you're professional about it," I said. I used Dean's word. "She's pretty fragile."

"She remember you from last year?" he asked. I'd told him about my one meeting with her.

"That's why Dean called me in," I said.

"What's his relationship with her?"

"He's known her a long time," I said. "They're friends."

"And not like Frank and she were friends, right?"

"Right."

"Okay, kiddo, fill me in."

I told him about my meeting with Marilyn that morning, and about the promises I made.

"Doesn't sound like you promised much more than that you'd try," Danny said. "She okay with that?"

"She was when I left her," I said.

"Okay, where do you want me? Vegas, or Tahoe?"

"Tahoe," I said. "Nose around, see if anybody's watching her cottage. I'll check the airport here, see if anyone was on her when she came in."

He knew my contacts at the airport were as good as his, maybe better, so he agreed.

"I'll get right on it, kid," he said. "I'll be in touch."

"Thanks, Danny."

"You'll get my bill."

"Yeah, right."

I wish he *would* bill me when he helped. I'd have the Sands pay him.

I broke the connection without hanging up, then called somebody I knew in security at McCarron Airport. I explained what I needed from him.

"Well, there sure were a bunch of folks watching that broad walk through the airport, Eddie," Ted Silver said. "I don't know how we could tell which one was followin' her."

"Do me a big favor, Teddy," I said. "I'd check with the cabbies myself but I'm jugglin' a lot of stuff here."

"I'm pretty busy, too, Eddie."

"Come on, be a pal," I said. "We've got a new blackjack dealer I think you might be able to handle."

"And I get the name after I do you this favor?"

"And tickets to a show, if you want."

"Sammy Davis this week?"

"I think I can do that. Actually, all three of them are here this week."

"Them other two guys are okay, but that Sammy. He's the best, and I ain't never seen him live."

"I'll arrange it."

"Okay, Eddie," he said, "lemme see what I can scare up for ya."

"Great, Teddy. Thanks."

I hung up and saw Marcy looking at me like I was crazy. I guess my voice must have gotten louder during the conversation.

"What?" I asked.

"Are you nuts?"

"Why?"

"You're gonna trust Danny Bardini around Marilyn Monroe?"

"Hey," I said, "if he couldn't handle you, he's not going to be able to handle her."

"Me?"

I walked behind her desk and leaned down to gather her into my arms.

"I've been alone in a room with Marilyn, and alone in a room with you," I whispered in her ear. "You've got it all over her."

"Me?"

"You."

I kissed her cheek. She blushed scarlet.

"Get out of here, Eddie," she said.

Seven

I STOPPED AT JACK Entratter's office to check in. His girl gave me a nod and told me to go ahead. She had never liked me and still didn't. I had learned to live with the disappointment.

"Eddie," Jack said, from behind his desk. "Have a seat."

I sat and asked, "Your nephew get in okay?"

"Yeah, the boy's here," he said. "He's visiting with my mother right now. What's goin' on with you and Dean?"

"Dean took me to Tahoe to see a friend of his."

He held up his hand before I could continue.

"And you're not gonna tell me who the friend is, are you?"

Dean hadn't told me not to, but it had become a habit with me to keep the Rat Pack's business to myself—even with Entratter. Besides, it had been my experience Jack always knew more than he was letting on.

"No, sir."

"You know, Eddie," he said. "This is about the only time I don't admire your loyalty."

"Yes, sir." I stood up. "I've got some things to do, so—"

"Sit down, Eddie," Entratter said. "I've got somethin' to talk to you about."

I sat back down.

"What's up, Jack?"

"You got a call while you were out," he said. "I took it."

"So?"

"It was from Brooklyn."

I hadn't been back to Brooklyn in many years—more than a dozen.

"What's it about, Jack?"

"Your mother died, Eddie."

"That's interesting."

Jack looked surprised. "That's not the reaction I expected."

"No, I wouldn't think so. I've observed that you're a real family man. You've even got your mother living here at the Sands with you."

"Well . . . she's got her own suite."

"I know," I said, "but if *my* mother was even living in the same town with me I'd kill myself."

"Don't you at least want to know who died?"

"I guess I don't have much choice, do I?"

When I left Brooklyn behind I left my family behind, too. There were good reasons for that. But when there's a death in the family everybody rallies, right?

After leaving Jack Entratter's office, I knew I'd have to fly back "home" for the funeral. I also knew I had to call someone and let them know I was coming.

But there was still a lot to do before addressing any of that. The funeral wouldn't be until the end of the week. My family couldn't have changed that much. So I had time to have dinner that night with Frank, Dean and Sammy.

Hopefully, I'd also have time to get some info from Teddy Silver at the airport, and from Danny when he went to Tahoe.

I took the elevator down to the lobby and made it to the casino floor before realizing I had automatically walked to my pit. It was three in the afternoon and even if I was keeping to my regular schedule it wouldn't be time for me to report in.

I decided I just had a lot on my mind at the moment and was kind of at a loss for something to do.

Or maybe the fact that my mother had died was hitting me harder than I thought it would.

Eight

I WENT TO THE SILVER QUEEN to get a drink. The bartender was new, aware of who I was, but unaware that this might be early for me to start drinking, so he just smiled and poured, which was good, because I probably would have bitten his head off if he'd gotten chatty.

I was in a foul mood.

I wasn't mad at Dean for getting me involved with Marilyn's problems. I wasn't upset with Marilyn. She couldn't help herself. I wasn't even mad at my boss, Jack, for taking the phone call from Brooklyn meant for me.

I guess the one I was mad at was my mother . . . for dying. And it wasn't even really for dying. We all have to go sometime. I was pissed because now I had to return to Brooklyn and see my family. Certainly not something I was looking forward to. When I'd left more than fourteen years ago, I'd never looked back.

I didn't feel I should be put in the position to have to explain myself. As far as I was concerned, I had had no other choice but to walk away—or run.

" 'Nother one?" the bartender asked.

"No, thanks."

I decided to go home for the rest of the day. I left a message for Dean that he and the guys should pick me up there.

I pulled into the driveway of my little house, turned off the Caddy and sat. I'd been living in that house since I became a pit boss at the Sands. When Jack Entratter bumped me up to the pit this was my only celebration of the promotion and raise. But it had never felt like home to me. The only place that felt like home was the Sands. Some people might think that was sad, but except for a few nights when I really needed to get away from the constant pulse of the strip, that casino was it. Lord knows the house I grew up in never felt like home.

I made a pot of coffee and a sandwich, and had them sitting at the kitchen table. I'd left both the Sands number and my home number with Teddy, but I knew he was right. With the number of people who would have been watching Marilyn in both airports, it'd be hard to tell if somebody was following her.

I doubted that Danny was even in Tahoe yet, so when the phone rang I almost didn't answer it, thinking it might be someone from Brooklyn. But in spite of myself, I walked to the counter and picked up the receiver.

"Eddie?"

The voice was low, tremulous but I recognized it right away.

"Marilyn?"

"I'm sorry to call you like this."

"No, no, it's okay," I said. I went back to the kitchen table and sat down, not knowing I'd be sitting there for a couple of hours.

The reason for the call didn't seem to be anything specific. She didn't ask if I'd found out anything, didn't refer to anything we'd talked about in cottage number three earlier that day. She seemed to need to talk, so we pretty much just shot the breeze for two hours. Now, if you'd told me the day before that I'd be shooting the breeze on the phone with Marilyn Monroe the next day I never would have believed it.

After two hours we both started to run down. Her words actually began to slur.

"I don't know why I don't have any real friends," she said. "I don't know why everybody thinks I'm hard to work with—"

"Marilyn, honey—"

"—but it's the other thing that really bothers me."

"What other thing?"

"The Clark Gable thing."

"You mean . . . the one about you bein' responsible for his death?"

"Yes."

"Marilyn, I thought we talked about that—"

"We did," she said, "but . . . it's still hard, having people say such horrible things. I guess I'm too sensitive."

"Marilyn, have you heard anyone gossiping about you and Clark Gable maybe having . . . an affair?"

"Eddie, no!" she said, adamant and breathy at the same time. "Clark loved his wife. He never did anything—"

"I'm not sayin' he did," I said. "I was just wonderin' . . . wouldn't that have bothered you more than . . . the other thing?"

"Oh Eddie," she said, "I've been gossiped about with so many men. Always accused of having sex with them. I'm used to it. But I've never been accused of causing someone's death."

"Marilyn, you did not cause Gable's death."

"But some people might think I did," she said. "Everyone loved Clark."

I heard something through the phone—maybe the sound of ice in a glass?

"Marilyn, are you drinkin'?"

"Just a little something to calm my nerves."

I didn't know if she had a serious drinking problem. I didn't rely on rumors and gossip for the truth, but her addictions had been front-page news for years.

"Well, don't have any more," I suggested. "You're not takin' anything else, are you?"

She laughed. "Oh, Eddie, do you think I'd mix booze and pills? That's dangerous."

"Marilyn, I just don't want you to do anything . . . silly."

"Well then," she said, "why don't you come over here and make sure I'm being a good girl?"

Jesus, did she mean what I thought she meant? Was Marilyn Monroe coming on to me? Was she inviting me over . . . for sex?

My first instinct was to rush right over there, but Dean had warned me how fragile she was. I had also seen it for myself, and now I was hearing it. She couldn't help but fall back on sex.

"Marilyn, you should get some rest."

I could hear the pout in her voice. "You don't want me, Eddie?"

"Every man wants you, Marilyn," I said. "Isn't that part of the problem?"

"Eddie, Eddie," she said. "Are you what I've been looking for all my life?"

"What's that?"

"A good man," she said, "a really good man?"

"Marilyn, Marilyn," I said, "I really don't think so."

She laughed and said, "Well, okay, then, you're an honest man."

"That I am," I said, and we both laughed.

"Marilyn, give me your phone number at home," I said. "I'm gonna see what I can find out regardin' Gable's death and get back to you."

"Okay, Eddie." She gave me the number that, last week, I wouldn't have believed I'd ever have.

"You're going home tomorrow?"

"Yes."

"I'll call you there, to make sure you're all right."

"Okay, Eddie," she said. "Dean was really right about you."

She hung up before I could ask the obvious question.

Nine

I HAD SHOWERED AND just finished dressing when I heard the horn out front. My neighbors had probably heard it, too. A big black limo was hugging the curb. I was sure people were watching as I got in the back. Dean, Frank and Sammy all slapped me on the back.

"How ya doin', Charley?" Sammy said.

"Good, Sam, it's great to see you guys. Where we goin'?"

"Where else?" Dean asked.

The Congo Room at the Sahara was a favorite place of Frank's. They kept a booth open there just for him.

"Tony and Janet are in town," Frank told me. "They're gonna meet us for dinner."

"Sounds good," I said. So that would be the night I met Tony Curtis and Janet Leigh. They were friends with Frank and Sammy. Dean's close friends, I knew, were few. He just didn't need people around him that much. He was happy with his family, or just alone. That was why he usually let Frank call the shots. It mattered to Frank.

The limo took us to the Sahara.

"First we're goin' into the Casbah Room to give Rickles a hard time," Frank said.

Frank liked Rickles, called him "Bullethead."

As soon as Rickles came out he targeted Frank, Sammy and Dean. I just happened to be sitting with them.

"Hey, guys, make yourselves comfortable," Rickles said. Then he held a make-believe tommy gun in his hands and went, "Rat-tat-tat-tat-tat-tat."

The guys started laughing, but then Frank stood up and said, "That's it, I'm gettin' outta here."

"Take it easy, Frank," Rickles said. "I have to listen to you sing."

"Jokes aside, kid," Frank said, "who's your favorite singer?"

Rickles immediately shot back, "Dick Haymes," and people were on the floor.

Suddenly Dean was on stage.

"I've got somethin' to say."

"Great," Rickles said, "the Pope speaks."

"Don Rickles is the funniest man in show business—but don't go by me, I'm drunk!"

When we got to the Congo Room, Tony and Janet had already been shown to Frank's booth. I found it hard not to stare at Janet Leigh. She was luminous. I'd had it bad for her ever since I saw her in *The Black Shield of Falworth* in 1954. Of course, Tony had the lead in that movie, and had uttered the famous words "Yonder lies the castle of my father," only with his Brooklyn accent he'd said "fadduh." Or so the joke goes. Actually, since I was from Brooklyn I knew he didn't have a Brooklyn accent. He was from the Bronx.

Peggy Lee was playing the Congo Room that night but we'd missed her set.

The introductions were made and when I said "Glad to meet

you," to them I was, of course, looking at Tony, trying not to stare at his wife.

The night was enjoyable, to say the least. Excellent food, good conversation. I was very happy to be sitting among those stars while other diners looked on. This was, to say the least, auspicious company.

It was Dean who called it quits first, saying he was going to head back to his suite at the Sands.

"Mind if I hitch a ride?" I asked.

"Oh, no, Charley, not you, too," Sammy said. "Come on, the night is young."

"I've got some things to do tomorrow, Sam," I said, "and I'll need to get an early start."

Sammy was going to tease me some more, but Frank put his hand on Sam's arm. I had the feeling Dean had told Frank about me helping Marilyn.

"Hey, Sam, leave the guy alone," Frank said. "Go on, Eddie. We understand."

I said my good-byes to Tony Curtis and Janet Leigh and then walked out with Dean, who was lucky enough to get a good-bye kiss from Janet. Dean had been in a film called *Who Was That Lady?* with both of them before he made *Ocean's Eleven*.

In the limo I told Dean about my conversations with Marilyn.

"You sendin' your buddy Danny to California with her?"

"Not exactly," I said. "He'll probably just tail her to the airport, see if anyone else is followin'. Then if we need to, I'm sure he knows somebody in L.A. who can watch her for us, but . . ."

"But what?"

"Marilyn's jumpy," I said. "We put a man on her and she might see him and get the wrong idea."

"That could push her over the edge."

"Whataya mean, push her over the edge?" I asked. "Dean, is she drinkin'? Doin' drugs?"

"To tell you the truth, Eddie, I'm not sure," Dean said, "but I wouldn't be surprised."

I rubbed my hand over my face, then over my hair, frustrated.

"What's on your mind, Eddie?" Dean asked. "There's somethin' more goin' on here. I saw it at dinner."

"Just family shit, Dean."

"Like what?"

I hesitated, then said, "I got a call from my sister . . . my mother died."

"Ah, geez, Eddie, I'm sorry, man. You didn't have to come out to dinner with us tonight."

"No, no, I wanted to," I said. "Look, I haven't seen any of my family in years. In fact, I haven't even called my sister back yet. But I'm probably gonna have to fly to New York, like, tomorrow. I'll make sure Marilyn can get hold of me if she has to."

"You're hooked, aren't you?" he asked.

"Dean, I didn't do anythin'—"

"No, no," he said, "I didn't mean that. I just meant hooked into her . . . vulnerability. Nothing sexual."

"Yeah. It's like you said it would be."

We pulled to a stop in front of the Sands. The chauffeur opened the door on Dean's side, but Dino signaled for him to close it again.

"Look, Eddie, you go to New York, do what you gotta do. Marilyn's not your responsibility. She's not anyone's, really, we just . . . her friends are worried."

"You asked me to talk with her and now I want to help her," I said. "If I fly to New York tomorrow I'll probably be back in three days. My family has never done anything slow, and I can't see that they've changed over the years. Today's Tuesday, my mother's probably bein' buried on Friday. Four days, then. No three. Ah hell, I'll be back probably Saturday."

"Look," Dean said, putting his hand on my arm, "take it

easy. Take care of family business and then come back. Everything will still be here. You comin' in?"

"No, I'm gonna go home."

"Billy'll drive you. See you when you get back, Eddie. I won't leave Vegas until Sunday."

"Okay, Dean. Thanks."

He slammed his door. The driver got back in, started the engine and pulled away. He turned on the radio. The sports report said Bob Feller and Jackie Robinson were being inducted into the Baseball Hall of Fame the next day.

Ten

I HEARD FROM TEDDY Silver as I was scraping dried eggs off a plate into the garbage after breakfast. It was one of the few times I tried cooking for myself, penance for all the time I spent eating out.

"Eddie?"

"Hey, Teddy."

"Hey, man, we got nothin'," he said. "She flew in here, and then on to Tahoe. A lot of us saw her, but there's no way we can tell if she was being followed. Just too damn many people."

"Okay, Teddy," I said. "That's what I figured. Thanks for tryin'."

"Sure, man. Hey, you gonna get to meet her?"

"Already have."

"Wow, man, that's, like, crazy. Is she as gorgeous up close and in person?"

"More, Teddy," I said, "much more."

"Damn—" he said, but I hung up before I could hear the rest.

Before I could make a move on my day the phone rang again.

"Eddie?"

"Hey, Danny."

"I'm here, man. She's inside. She never left the room all night." I heard him yawn.

"How do you know for sure?"

"I talked to a desk clerk, and took a peek in a window," he said. "I saw her there. She looks so small . . . so sad."

Even Danny, I thought. Biggest hound I ever knew, and he could see it.

"Okay, Danny. She's headin' home today, I think."

"You want me to go with her?"

"All the way to L.A.?"

"I thought you wanted her watched?"

"Just see if anyone follows her as far as McCarron," I said. "From there you can make up your own mind."

"Do you think she's imaginin' it?" Danny asked. "Or do you think it's for real?"

"I talked to her for a while yesterday," I said. "I'm afraid she's imaginin' the whole thing, Danny."

"Maybe," Danny said, "but it's real to her, ya know?"

"Yeah, pal," I said, "I'm afraid I do know. Look, man, I think I'm gonna be flyin' home for a few days."

"Home?" Danny asked. "You mean, Brooklyn? What for?"

"My mother died."

Danny was quiet. He knew my mom when we were kids.

"Eddie, I'm sorry . . . who called?"

"My sister."

"You talked to her?"

"Not yet. I'm gonna call her . . . well, probably when I hang up on you."

"This is a bummer, man. You and your family . . ."

"Yeah, I know."

"Look, if you're gonna be in New York you want me to follow Marilyn all the way home?"

"That'll cost," I said. "A plane ticket, someplace to stay for a few days . . ."

"That's okay," Danny said. "I'll bill ya."

I hesitated, then said, "You know what? Yeah, okay, do it. Keep a close eye on her. I'm afraid she's drinkin', or worse."

"Drugs?"

"Maybe."

"Okay, Eddie," Danny said. "I got your back, man."

"I know you do, Danny. You always do."

"Fuckin' A."

After I hung up on Danny I made the call I'd been dreading since yesterday.

"Hello?"

"Hello, Angie."

I could hear my sister catch her breath. "Eddie?"

"Yeah, it's me. I got your message."

"I wasn't sure—I didn't think you'd call."

"Why'd you call me, then?"

Angie hesitated, then said, "She was your mother, too."

"Yeah," I said. "When did she die?"

"Yesterday. I called right aw—as soon as I could."

"When's the wake?"

"The next two nights," she said. "Then we'll bury her on Thursday."

Two nights. Great.

"You're not comin', are you?" she asked.

"Again," I said, "if you don't want me to come, why did you call?"

She became impatient with me, sounded like the sister I remembered.

"I was just tryin' to do the right thing, Eddie."

"Did you tell him you called me?"

"Hell, no," she said. "I didn't tell nobody, not even Tony."

Tony was her husband, my asshole brother-in-law. My family was always such a cliché.

"Not Joey?" My brother, another a-hole.

"No."

"Okay, Ang," I said.

"That's all you gotta say?"

"Yeah, right now," I said. "Thanks for lettin' me know."

"You wanna know what she died of?"

"Sure."

"Cancer," my sister said. "It ate her up."

I rubbed my forehead. My father would say she died of a broken heart, and it was my fault. See what I mean? Cliché. An Italian family is an Italian family.

"I'll see you, Ang," I said.

"Are you comin'—" she started to say, but I hung up.

Eleven

TALKING WITH MY SISTER had been . . . unsettling. Unpleasant, even, but then it always had been. Same with the rest of my family. That's what happens when you're the only sane member.

But I still had to go back and for that I needed a plane ticket. Trying to get a ticket to fly the same day would cost an arm and a leg. I needed help getting one on the cheap, especially since Danny had probably already blown a wad, and was going to bill me for it.

I went to the Sands, waved at Jack's girl in passing and entered his office.

"Eddie—"

"I need your help, Jack. I've got to fly to New York today."

"Not in the chopper—"

"No, I don't need the chopper, I need a plane ticket—a cheap plane ticket. So could you pick up the phone and do what you do?"

"Do what I do?"

"You know, that Entratter stuff you do. Exert your influence, bully people . . . whatever."

"Bully people?"

"Yeah, you bully people, Jack . . . sometimes."

He stared at me, then said, "Yeah, you're right." He picked up the phone. "When do you wanna leave?"

Jack let me make one call before I left to go to McCarran to catch my flight.

Luckily, they had flights going to New York almost every hour. I had packed a light bag that morning and carried it with me when I got to La Guardia.

My ride was waiting at the terminal. He hadn't been hard to spot. He was wearing a black-and-white checkerboard sports jacket, black slacks, a white shirt and a matching checked tie. The tops of his black shoes also had checks on them.

"Hey, Mr. G.," Jerry greeted me.

"Thanks for pickin' me up, Jerry."

"What're friends for? Lemme get that." He took my bag. "My car's this way."

As I followed him I realized this was the first time he'd ever referred to us as friends. It was nice, but I still wasn't sure he wouldn't whack me in a minute on Frank Sinatra or MoMo Giancana's say-so.

A snazzy-looking '59 Caddy was parked in a No Parking Zone. I didn't bother asking how he got away with that.

"Nice car," I said.

"Thanks, but it ain't as nice as yours." He dumped my bag in the backseat.

Mine was a '53 in mint condition, a replacement for my '52 that had been blown up with me inside. But that story's been told.

"Where to, Mr. G.?"

Where to stay? I hadn't thought that far ahead.

"I don't know yet, Jerry. Let's just drive."

"Sure thing."

As he blew through traffic, getting out of the airport, he asked, "What brings you to New York, Mr. G.? You didn't say on the phone."

"A funeral, Jerry."

"Whose?"

"My mother's."

"Aw, geez, Mr. G. Sorry."

"Hey, Jerry."

"Yeah?"

"Since we're friends, and we've known each other two years now, do you think you could start callin' me Eddie?"

He thought a moment, then said, "I dunno, Mr. G. I'll have to give it some thought."

"Okay, big guy," I said. "You do that."

We approached the highway as he asked, "Can you tell me if we're goin' to Manhattan or Brooklyn?"

"The funeral's in Brooklyn, but I'm still not sure where I'm stayin'."

"You ain't stayin' with your family?"

"Noooo," I said, very definitely.

"Okay, then," he said, taking the ramp to Brooklyn, "yer stayin' with me."

"Hey, Jerry, you don't have to do—"

Cutting me off, he said, "It gives us someplace ta go, and you can change yer mind later if ya want. Besides, I got plenty of room."

"Okay, Jerry, thanks."

"And how about we get a pizza on the way?" he asked. "Bet you ain't had Brooklyn pizza in years."

"Jerry," I said, "that sounds like a damn good idea."

Twelve

WE STOPPED OFF FOR PIZZA and a couple of six-packs of Ballantine beer, then drove to Jerry's apartment, which was in Sheepshead Bay.

We parked in a carport behind the building and went up a flight of stairs.

"I got the whole top floor," he said, as he unlocked the door. "You can smell the water from here, and you can see the bay from the roof. It's only a couple of blocks away."

Sheepshead Bay was home to fishing boats that went out every morning and came back every evening with their catch, as well as shops and restaurants that depended on the fishing. I'd spent a lot of time there as a teenager, and enjoyed many meals in Lundy's, a Brooklyn landmark that seated as many as 2,400 people, as well as Randazzo's Clam Bar, the best place for clams in Brooklyn.

We entered through the kitchen, put the pizza and beer down on a yellow Formica-topped table.

"It ain't fancy," Jerry said. "Just a living room, bedroom, kitchen and bathroom, but it's enough for me."

"I don't want to crowd you, Jerry . . ."

"I got a big sofa, Mr. G.," Jerry said. "You don't mind slee-pin' on it, you ain't gonna crowd me."

He retrieved two mismatched plates from a cabinet, set them on the table, and opened both pizza boxes. One was plain cheese, the way I liked it, the other pepperoni, for Jerry. We sat, popped the tops on some beers, and dug in. Jerry was right, it had been years since I'd had Brooklyn pizza. It was even better than I remembered.

"I was surprised when you called, Mr. G.," Jerry said. "Ain't nobody in your family got a car?"

"I don't get along so well with my family, Jerry," I said. "Haven't for a very long time. That's why I called you. I just . . . needed somebody I could count on. You're the only person in New York who fit the bill."

"Wow," Jerry said. "That's, like . . . okay, Mr. G. You know you can count on me. You want me to drive you to the funeral home?"

I took a second slice of pizza.

"That's what I was thinkin', Jerry, but now I'm not so sure I want to go. Not tonight."

"Okay, so, tomorrow, then?"

"Maybe," I said.

"I mean . . . you flew all the way here, and not to go?"

"I'll go Thursday," I said. "For the actual burial, but the wake—you know, that's just a bunch of people who haven't seen each other since the last funeral."

"Ya know," Jerry said, "sometimes I think those wakes—people use them as family reunions."

"Exactly," I said, "only it's a bunch of people gathered to-gether who don't really want to see one another, other than at funerals."

"I know what ya mean, Mr. G.," Jerry said.

I grabbed a third piece while Jerry had a fourth, a second beer while he had a third.

"Jerry, we've never talked about your family," I said.

"Ain't got one, Mr. G. I spent time in foster homes, then boys' homes, reform schools, then prison. But I been on my own now for twenty years."

"You were never adopted?"

"I was too bad to be adopted," Jerry said. "I knew that. I never took it personal when they sent me back to the home."

"Maybe you were better off," I said. "You didn't have crazy parents playin' with your head."

"That's what happened to you?"

"Me, my brother, my sister."

"Wow, I didn't know you had no brother an' sister, Mr. G."

"Yeah, but they didn't make it out like I did," I said. "They're as crazy as the people who raised us."

"Your father," Jerry asked. "Is he still alive?"

"Oh, yeah . . ."

"So you'll see him at the funeral."

"Yes."

I used a napkin to clean grease from my chin, then drank some beer. Pizza and beer, such simple pleasures, reminding me of the good parts of my youth in Brooklyn.

"I'm not lookin' forward to it."

"But you gotta do it, right?" Jerry asked. "Because she was your mother?"

"That's the only reason I flew here," I said. "Because I had to."

That reminded me. I had to call the Sands, let them know how to get in touch with me.

"Can I use your phone to call Vegas?"

"Sure, Mr. G. It's right there."

Jack's girl made me wait, but finally put me through to him.

"I'm at this number, Jack," I said, reading the digits off the dial.

"What hotel is that?"

"I'm . . . stayin' with a friend."

"Not family?"

"Hell, no."

"Okay, Eddie," Entratter said. "I hope it's not all too . . . bad for you."

"Thanks, Jack. I'm sure I'll be back by Friday."

"Okay."

Next I called Danny's office, got Penny, his secretary.

"Eddie, where have you been?" she asked.

"Busy. Is he around?"

"No, he's in L.A."

"He is? Still?"

"Well, you gave him permission to tail Marilyn Monroe. I think he's taking full advantage of it."

"Is somethin' wrong?"

"Not that I know of."

"Okay, if he wants to talk to me he can get me here." Once again, I read the number off the center of the dial.

"What hotel is that?"

"Why does everybody want me to spend money on a hotel?" I asked. "I'm stayin' with a friend."

"Not family?"

"Good-bye, Penny."

I looked at Jerry, who had one slice of pizza left in his box. There were four still in mine. I went over and picked one up.

"Startin' already, huh?" he asked.

"What?"

"All the questions."

"Questions I don't want to answer."

"I know," Jerry said. "People used ta ask me about my family all the time. They wuz always shocked to find out I didn't have one. Guineas, they got so many family members, ya know? Oops, sorry, Mr. G."

"That's okay, Jerry," I said. "I know Italian families are large.

Nothin' I can do about that. All I can do is steer clear of the crazy."

"So you moved to Vegas," Jerry said. "No crazy there, right?"

I bit into my pizza. "At least I'm not related to it."

Thirteen

I SPENT THE FIRST DAY of the wake in front of Jerry's TV.

After we finished most of the pizza and all of the beer he asked me what I wanted to do. I told him I didn't want to hold him up, that if he had business he needed to take care of, go ahead.

"I got nothin' doin', Mr. G.," he said. "I'm pretty much free and clear for a coupla days, at least."

"Well, you don't have to entertain me, Jerry."

"You just lost yer mother, so I feel kinda, ya know, obligated ta at least sit with ya."

"Well, that's nice but—"

"I think I got a bottle of bourbon around here, someplace," he said. "We could watch some TV."

"That doesn't sound too bad," I said. "Sort of our own private wake right here—at least, for a while."

So we drank bourbon—Jack Daniel's—and watched television. I was having a much better time than I would have had at the funeral parlor, trying to defend my life to my family.

Next thing I knew it was morning, and I was sprawled on the couch. There was a pillow under my head, and a blanket draped over me. I could smell coffee and bacon. I sat up, bumping into a coffee table that stood right in front of the sofa.

"You got time to jump inta the shower, Mr. G. I put fresh towels in there for ya. I'm makin' omelets. Ya want toast with yours?"

God, he sounded perky—not a word I would have previously associated with Big Jerry. If I didn't know better I'd think he was happy to have the company.

"Toast would be good," I said. "I'll be quick."

I grabbed my toiletries from my bag and stumbled into the bathroom. It was small, stark, very white. It smelled as if it had recently been cleaned. In the shower I found a fresh bar of soap next to a bottle of shampoo. There was also a bottle of something that seemed to be for the treatment of thinning hair. Was Jerry concerned about a receding hairline?

Used the soap, my own shampoo, got dressed and shuffled to the kitchen with damp hair.

"Just in time," Jerry said. He put a mug of coffee in front of me. No milk, no sugar, which meant he remembered how I took it. Food was always a main concern with Jerry, so he obviously had a good memory about it.

He put a plate on the table piled with a stack of white toast, and then set two plates of omelets down. I could see green peppers, onions and bacon in the eggs.

"You want hot sauce or somethin'?" he asked.

"No, this is great. You didn't have to do this."

"I don't mind. I like cookin'. Ya probably wanna have a diner breakfast while you're here, though, so we can do that tomorrow."

As with the pizza I hadn't been to a Brooklyn Greek diner in a long time. I hadn't thought about it, but he was right. I would like a diner breakfast before I went back to Vegas. Who knew if I'd ever be back to Brooklyn after this? That depended on how I got along with my father, my brother and my sister. If things went as badly as I expected them to, I knew I'd never be back, no matter what.

I added salt and pepper to my omelet, which Jerry didn't seem to mind. He did the same with his. I buttered some toast to go with it.

"Hey, I forgot," he said, getting up quickly. He came back with a pitcher of orange juice he'd obviously prepared earlier.

"Well," I said, as he poured two glasses, "now it's perfect. Thanks, Jerry."

"Sure, Mr. G."

"I guess I'm kind of surprised you didn't make pancakes."

"Pancakes is my thing," he said. "You're my guest."

"You, uh, entertain often?"

"Naw," he said, "never."

He was a pretty good host for somebody who never had company.

After breakfast Jerry cleaned his kitchen while I went into the living room to watch some TV. When he was done he came in and sat with me.

"You goin' to the wake today, Mr. G.?"

"I don't know, Jerry," I said. "I haven't decided."

"Whataya wanna do today, then?"

I had been thinking about that while I was watching television.

"I'll tell you what I wanna do," I said. "I wanna walk down to the bay, take a look at the boats, walk past Lundy's and some of the other old hangouts, and end up at Randazzo's for some clams for lunch. How's that sound?"

"Didja bring a coat from Vegas?" Jerry asked. "It's gonna be cold today."

"I did remember that it was winter in New York, Jerry," I said.

Fourteen

I HADN'T REALLY PACKED a coat, but I did bring some thermal underwear to go under the jacket I had brought, as well as a heavy sweatshirt. When I was properly layered I was ready to go. Jerry donned a long overcoat, and we left his place to walk the two blocks down to the bay.

The layering just barely worked, but I wasn't about to complain to Jerry that I was cold. It was too early for Lundy's to be open, but walking by the building did make me feel kind of nostalgic for my misspent youth.

We walked down by the water. Most of the boats had gone out already, and wouldn't be back until dinnertime. My brother and I had worked on some of the boats for a few years. That was back when we were still kind of friendly, before he became a crazy clone of my father.

By lunchtime I was almost frozen, so the inside of Randazzo's Clam Bar was a welcome relief. We split a huge order a clams and washed it down with beer. Jerry asked me what was going on in Vegas.

"Seen much of Mr. S., or Dino lately? Or any of those guys?"

"As a matter of fact," I said, "Frank, Dean and Sammy are in Vegas now, playin' the Sands." I told him about having dinner with them, and meeting Tony Curtis and Janet Leigh.

"She was in *Prince Valiant*, right?"

"That's right."

"She's a real babe," he said. "Ya know, them pointy tits."

"I know, Jerry."

"Any trouble with them guys?"

"No, but . . ."

"But what?"

I figured, what the hell? I was in Brooklyn and Marilyn was in L.A.

"Dean did ask me to see if I could help out a friend of his."

"Who?"

"Marilyn Monroe."

His jaw dropped—which wasn't pretty, because he had a mouthful of clams.

"Yer shittin' me!"

"No."

"You met her?"

"I went to Tahoe—remember the Cal Neva Lodge in Tahoe? Well, she was stayin' in one of those cabins."

"You was in a cabin alone with her? Is she a nympho like they say? Did she jump ya?"

"I'm sorry to disappoint you, Jerry," I said, "but she didn't jump me. She's more of a scared kid than a nympho."

"What's got her scared?"

"Well, for one thing, folks are sayin' she caused the death of Clark Gable while they were makin' *The Misfits*."

"That's crazy," he said. "Gable was an old guy doin' his own stunts. I read about all that stuff. Sure, she kept 'em waitin' a lot in the desert—but how could that kill him? Don't they have fancy, air-conditioned dressing rooms?"

"That's just what I told her, Jerry."

"Jeez, folks are mean, ya know?"

"Yeah, I do know."

"So, whataya gonna do for her?"

"I don't know, really. I've already spent time on the phone, kinda talkin' her down. Right now I got Danny keepin' an eye on her. She seems to think she was bein' followed."

"Lucky dog," Jerry said. "I mean, followin' behind Marilyn Monroe. Ya know, because of that ass—"

"I get it, Jerry," I said. "I get it."

We finished our clams and I paid the tab, then we walked back to Jerry's place. I took off my jacket, but he left his coat on.

"Mr. G., I gotta go down the street and pick up my laundry, and then I gotta make another stop. Ya wanna come along?"

"No, Jerry, that's okay," I said. "I told you, I don't wanna mess with your routine. Just go and do what you gotta do. I'll be fine."

"Okay, Mr. G." He headed for the door, then stopped. "I'll be walkin', so the car keys'll be here in case ya wanna, you know, go somewheres."

"Thanks, Jerry."

He nodded and left. I turned the TV on and sat down to watch, but I wasn't concentrating. I looked at my watch. If I drove over to the funeral home now I'd find everybody there. There'd be crying, and some laughing, funny stories to tell. Only when I walked in, it would all stop. They'd stare at me as I walked up to the coffin and looked down at my mother. Then there'd be some snide remarks, mostly behind my back, some to my face. My father probably wouldn't even talk to me.

When the phone rang I jumped, then felt silly. I picked it up after the second ring. Probably for Jerry, anyway.

"Hello?"

"Eddie, is that you?"

"Penny? Yeah, it's me. What's wrong?"

"Maybe nothing, but . . ."

"Go ahead."

"I haven't heard from Danny," she said. "I—I can't get ahold of him."

"Is he still in L.A.?"

"Supposed to be."

"Was he stayin' at a hotel?"

"He got a cheap motel room near where Marilyn lives," she said. "I've been calling, but there's no answer. I've left several messages."

"All of this yesterday and today?"

"Yes. Eddie, I'm sorry to call you at a time like this. I mean, with your mother and all, but—"

"It's okay, Penny," I said. "Look, the funeral's tomorrow. I'll head back right after that. Don't worry, I'll find out what's goin' on."

"I was probably silly to call you," she said. "I could've just called a local PI out there, have them check—"

"Okay, do that," I said, "but I'm still comin' back. I'll see you tomorrow."

"Okay, Eddie."

She started to hang up and I said, "Penny, wait a minute?"

"I'm here."

"Let me have the phone number of Danny's motel," I said. "I'll keep tryin' him there."

"Good idea," she said, and read it off to me.

"Thanks, Eddie," she said. "I—I feel better after talking to you."

I hung up, not knowing why she felt better. I really hadn't told her anything that would make her less fearful. I knew Danny could take care of himself, but he usually checked in with Penny when he was away. If anything had happened to him it would be my fault—only what could have happened? All he did was follow Marilyn home.

Unless . . . unless Marilyn was being followed, as she suspected, and Danny had run into whoever it was.

Fifteen

JERRY CAME BACK a couple of hours later during a commercial for Chunky Chocolate Bars. I turned off the TV and told him about the phone call. I had to talk to somebody about it, and anyway, it was better than trying to make inane conversation in order to avoid talking about the funeral.

Jerry listened, nodding the whole time, not interrupting.

"She was gonna call a PI from L.A. to check it out?" he asked, when I was done.

"Yeah, that's what she was thinking. But I'm thinking I'll find him."

"Then we will, Mr. G.," Jerry said. "We'll find him."

"You're probably right," I said, "but Danny . . . he's . . ."

"I know," Jerry said. "He's your friend. You can worry, if ya want, but ya ain't gonna know nothin' for sure—at least, not until tomorrow."

"With all the craziness in my family, Jerry, Danny's like . . . the last family I have."

"I know, Mr. G. I know."

"But you're right," I said. "There's nothing I can do now."

"What about the funeral, Mr. G.?"

"Why do you keep askin' me about it, Jerry?"

"Because I think you're thinkin' about not goin'."

"So?"

"So you flew all this way. Yer gonna kick yourself if ya don't go."

He was right. I was thinking about not going at all, especially after the call about Danny. My return ticket was for Friday, I could change it to Thursday with no problem. But I could change it and still make my mother's funeral.

"Listen, Mr. G.," Jerry said, "I don't like flyin', but I do it a lot. Like when I fly out to Vegas when you call me. So I got a travel agent takes care of all that for me an' I don't gotta bother. I could call 'im and—"

"Okay, go ahead," I said. "Call him."

"Whataya wanna do?"

"My mother's funeral is tomorrow mornin'," I said. "Change my flight to tomorrow afternoon. I'll head back right after the funeral."

"That's good, Mr. G. Gimme your ticket."

I got my ticket out of my jacket pocket and handed it over. He dialed the phone, then waited for it to be picked up.

"This is a good idea, Mr. G. Believe me, if ya didn't go—hey, Artie? Jerry Epstein. I need a favor . . ."

As always, since I'd met him, Jerry proved he wasn't as dumb as he liked people to think he was.

After he hung up he handed back my ticket.

"He's makin' the change. You can show that at the ticket desk and they'll give ya a new one."

"Thanks, Jerry."

"I can drive ya to the funeral tomorrow, Mr. G., and then take ya right to La Guardia. Or . . ."

"Or what?"

He looked at the clock.

"I could drive ya over there tonight," he said.

"Tonight?"

"I'll even go in with ya," he said. "How's that?"

At first it sounded like my idea of hell, but then I thought about the look on my sister's face when I walked in with Jerry.

"You know what?" I said. "Let's do it. Maybe you don't play host very often, but you make a damn good one."

"Hey, I learned from you, Mr. G.," he said with a smile. "You always show me a good time when I come to Vegas."

Yeah, I thought, but at least I never had to kill anybody.

Sixteen

I WAS THE CENTER of attention as soon as I entered LaPolla's Funeral Home on Rockaway Parkway in Canarsie. Of course, it helped that Jerry came in with me, wearing a houndstooth jacket, which he said was the closest thing he had to black.

Cousins shook my hand and asked how the hell I was.

My brother and brother-in-law stayed on the other side of the room, glowering.

My sister had a tissue to her face, looked like she had just finished crying. When she saw me she started all over again.

"There's a lot of people here," Jerry said.

"And this looks like only half the family."

"They don't seem so crazy," he said.

"Wait for it."

"Your cousins seem nice. How many you got?"

"About thirty-two."

"Huh?" He looked shocked.

My father was sitting in the front row. He turned to see what the hubbub was all about. When we locked eyes he got up and came over to me. He'd aged badly, the skin on his face sagging, his clothes hanging on a frame that while no means thin, was not as bulky as it once was. And he was smaller than I remembered. Even though I'd left New York when I was in my late twenties and a man myself, he'd always made me feel like a small boy in his presence. But when he took my face in his hands I could still feel the strength. That hadn't changed.

"I'm so glad you came, son," he said. He shocked me by kissing me on the cheek, and then hugging me.

"My boy, my boy," he kept saying.

Over his shoulder I could see Jerry watching us. I'm sure he was wondering where the crazy was.

Wait for it, I thought again.

My father stopped hugging and held me at arm's length. My sister moved up alongside him.

"You look good, boy," he said. "Doesn't he look good, Angie?"

"Yes, he does, Poppa," she said. "He looks good."

My sister was the baby of the family, but while I knew she was thirty, she looked like she was in her forties. Her face was lined, her hands rough, and she wore very little makeup.

My father held my shoulders a little longer, his eyes wet, and then I saw it. For years I called it "the change." My father changed his "tune." His attitude could turn on a dime. Sometimes it happened when he was out of the room. One version of my father would leave and moments later the new version would enter. But every so often it happened in front of us. We could see it, and prepare for it.

He slapped my upper arms and said, "Are you happy now that you killed your mother?"

The room got quiet. I could still see Jerry behind my father, and he looked as if he'd just been slapped.

"Why don't you go and look at her?" my father shouted. "Take a look at your handiwork!"

I turned to my sister. She did what my mother had always

done when I looked to her for help. She shrugged helplessly. I grew up with a crazy man, a bully, knowing before I could talk that my mother would never be there for me. Once she mouthed the words, "I'm sorry," during one of my father's tirades, but that was the most I ever got from her.

My brother came over and stood next to my father.

"Why don't you go take a look, *brother*?" he asked.

Joey was older than me by two years. Early in my childhood I realized I was different. Nobody was on my side. I usually took the brunt of my father's anger, even if I had nothing to do with the reason he was so mad. Joey always took such delight in the fact that I was the target, and it was always very important to him that my father know he was there, on *his* side. I always felt that as brothers, it should've been us against my old man, but that had never been the case.

"Go on," Joey said. "Look at her."

"She's been dying since the day you left," my father said. "I'm surprised it took this long."

Tears were streaming down my sister's face, but she remained silent. My cousins, aunts and uncles found something else to look at. When my father got like this, nobody got in his way.

"If anybody killed her it was you, old man," I said. "Living with you."

"Your mother was happy with me," he said. "It was only when you kids came along—" He stopped short. "When *you* came along—"

I looked at my sister, and then my brother.

"Are you listenin' to this?" I asked them.

My sister hid behind her tissues.

My brother hid behind his bluster.

"It broke her heart when you left!" Joey said. "We stayed." He looked at my father. "We stayed, Poppa."

"Oh, shut up," my father said. "You all killed her. I don't care about any of you. But you—"

All of a sudden he drew back his fist and I knew I was going to take the hit for everybody. There was no way I'd ever hit him back, and why I didn't think to block the blow is beyond me. But his fist never reached me because Jerry reached out and caught my father's arm by the wrist. My old man tried to pull away, but Jerry was too strong.

"You brought a hoodlum with you to attack our father?" my sister shrieked. "Tony! Tony!"

She was yelling for her husband, my brother-in-law, but he was too much of a coward to come anywhere near Jerry. He stayed where he was across the room.

No one else rushed forward, either. Jerry was just too imposing a figure.

"Mr. G.?" he asked me. "Ya want I should snap it?"

I didn't know if he meant the wrist or the whole arm, but I didn't want either. And truth be told, after my father berated me in front of the entire family—or half the family—I was kind of ticked at my mother all over again for all the times she never stood up to him. I didn't particularly want to go up to her casket to see her.

"No," I told Jerry, "let him go."

He released my father's wrist and the old man stepped back, rubbing it, warily regarding Jerry.

"Get out, Eddie," my brother said, "and take your hood with you."

"You want I should bust him up, Mr. G.?" Jerry asked, pointing at my brother, who shrank back as if he thought I was going to sic the big boy on him.

I was tempted.

"No, that's okay, Jerry."

"Then why don't we get outta here, Mr. G.?" Jerry suggested.

"I'm with you, Jerry. Let's go."

Under the watchful eye of everyone Jerry and I left.

Out in the parking lot Jerry said, "Geez, Mr. G., I'm sorry."

"For what? You didn't do anythin'."

"I made you come here," Jerry said. "You're right, those people are nuts."

"Yeah, they are," I said. "They sure are."

The next day Jerry drove me to the cemetery at the very end of the procession of cars. I stood off to the side during the ceremony while he waited in the Caddy. Then I walked to the car. We were the first ones to drive away.

To La Guardia, and back to Vegas.

Back to my life.

My Vegas, where the people tryin' to kill you were the bad guys—not family.

Seventeen

THE TICKET CHANGE WENT smoothly. I slept through most of the flight, dreaming that I was in Coney Island with my brother, Danny, and Danny's brother, Nick, my best friend. We were eating Nathan's hot dogs. I woke up wondering why I hadn't had Jerry drive me there before we left.

I was walking through McCarran when I felt a heavy hand come down on my shoulder. It was a very familiar pressure.

"Hey, Mr. G.," Jerry said.

"Where did you come from?"

"Seven rows behind you."

"No, I mean—"

"I know what ya mean, Mr. G.," Jerry said. "I figured you could use some help on this one."

"On which one?"

"Yer missin' friend," he said, "not to mention Marilyn Monroe."

"How the hell did I miss you on the plane?" I asked. The question was more for me than him.

"You never looked," he said. "And you slept most of the way. Come on, Mr. G. Did ya leave your car here?"

"No," I said, "we'll have to take a cab."

He gave me a look I've seen on lots of puppies over the years.

"You ain't sorry ta see me, are ya?"

"No, Jerry," I said. "I'm not sorry to see you. Come on, we're goin' to the Sands first to get you a room."

"We ain't stayin' at your house?"

"Naw," I said, "I could never match your hospitality. This time, I'm gettin' you a suite!"

We arrived at the Sands and I got Jerry situated in a suite. I told him I didn't need him because I was going to see Jack Entratter, so he figured he'd just take a shower and enjoy the place.

"Order room service," I suggested.

"Really? What can I get?"

"Anything."

After I left him I wondered if I'd just opened a can of worms I'd never be able to close.

"Welcome back, Eddie," Entratter said, as I entered his office. "How was the—I mean, how did it go?"

"It went," I said. "Listen, Jack, I may have to leave again. If I do it'll be quick."

"Where to this time?"

"L.A."

"This have to do with that favor for Dean?"

I nodded. It was actually Danny, but that name didn't carry the same weight.

"Okay, Eddie," he said, "just keep me informed."

"Will do, Jack."

I started to leave, then stopped.

"Jack, are the guys still in town?"

"Dean is," he said. "Sammy had to leave, and Frank went to Palm Springs. He's still havin' that construction done."

"Dean in the same suite?"

"Yeah. You wanna go see 'im?"

"Yeah, right now."

"I'll call 'im and set it up," Entratter said. "Just go on up."

"Thanks, Jack."

Dean opened the door. "Hey, pally, how are ya?"

"I'm okay, Dean," I said, entering the room.

"The funeral?" He closed the door and turned to face me. He was dressed casually, cream-colored slacks and a yellow pull-over short-sleeved shirt with a collar. Cream-colored loafers matched the pants.

"Over with," I said. "I'm not here to talk about that, though."

"Okay," he said. "Drink?"

"Where's Mack?"

"Didn't make the trip this time," Dean said. "I can get you a drink myself, though."

"Too early," I said.

He walked to the bar, where a glass filled with a clear liquid and ice sat. I knew from past experience it was soda water.

"I appreciate you stayin' over, Dean."

"I told you I wouldn't leave 'til you got back," he said. "Gave me time to get some golf in. What's on your mind now?"

"Marilyn thinks she's being followed," I said. "What do you think?"

"What I always think," he said. "She's a frightened, confused child in a woman's body."

"Well, maybe she's right, this time," I said.

"How do you mean?"

"Can I use your phone?"

"Sure, go ahead. It's your hotel. Make it long distance if you want."

"No, that's okay," I said. "Local is good."

I dialed the number of Danny's office and waited for Penny to pick up. I let it ring a dozen times, but there was no answer.

"Okay," I said, hanging up, "now I'm really worried."

"What's goin' on, buddy?"

"My friend, Danny, followed Marilyn to L.A. to make sure she was safe," I said, "and now he's missing."

"How do you know that?"

"His secretary called me in New York, said she hadn't heard from him, and couldn't get ahold of him. Now I just called his office, and she didn't answer."

"So you think she's missing?"

"Maybe she's out to lunch," I said, "but I've got to go and find out. After that, I'm pretty sure I'll be goin' to L.A. Look, Dean, I know you've got things to do. I don't expect you to hang around here."

"I'm gonna leave tomorrow, as a matter of fact," he said, "but I'm gonna give you my home number, and my manager's number. Keep me informed, all right? And let me know if I can do anything."

"Will do," I said, shaking his hand. "Thanks, Dean."

"No, thank you," he said, walking me to the door. "You're only involved in this because I asked you."

"Well, now I'm involved because I'm concerned about Marilyn," I said, "and my friends."

I left to go and get Jerry. It looked like I might be needing him after all.

Eighteen

I PICKED JERRY UP and as we walked to the parking lot I explained the situation. He drove the Caddy, and I was impressed that he remembered the way to Danny's office. When I asked Jerry to park in front of Danny's building he insisted on parking down the street, "Just in case."

We walked back to Danny's office. The downstairs door was unlocked, but that wasn't unusual. We also found the upstairs door unlocked, which it usually was during business hours.

"You got your gun?" I asked Jerry.

"You bet." He pulled his jacket aside to show me the .45 under his arm, but he didn't draw it.

As we entered we saw the outer office was empty.

"Penny?" I called. She could have been in Danny's office, but there was no answer. Jerry went and checked it anyway.

"Empty," he said. "Maybe she went out for tea?"

Again I was impressed that he remembered Penny drank tea. It had taken me years to get that straight.

"Maybe, but . . ."

"But what?"

"Somethin' doesn't feel right."

"Like what?"

I walked to Danny's office and looked inside. The top of his desk was a mess. Danny always said his desk looked like the inside of his head.

On the other hand, Penny's desk was always clean and neat. Only now there were letters sprawled across it and pencils strewn about, rather than in her pencil mug.

"Somebody took her," I said.

"How do you know?"

I pointed at her desk and explained. "She's sendin' us a message."

Jerry walked to the window and stared down at Fremont Street. Then he looked directly across, at the windows on the other side of the street.

"I don't see nothin'." He turned to face me. "Whataya wanna do? Call the cops?"

"I wouldn't know what to tell them," I said. "Her desk is a little messy. What would that mean to them? Besides, a great man once told me no good ever came from callin' the cops," I added, quoting him.

"You know where she lives?" Jerry asked.

"No."

"Well, we can find the address somewhere here," he said.

I scratched my head.

"I guess we should check her place. She's probably listed in the phone book."

We looked around, located the phone book and looked up her number. I dialed and she answered on the second ring.

"Penny?"

"Eddie? Where are you?"

"Your office. I thought—"

"You thought what? I'm upset, I didn't want to sit in the office all day. I'm not going in until Danny comes back. Eddie, what's going on? Why didn't you call me when you got back?"

"Penny, I came lookin' for you at the office. When I saw the mess on your desk I thought . . . I thought you were missing, too."

"That's sweet, Eddie, that you were worried, but I'm fine. I just left in a hurry. I had to get out of there."

"I understand, honey."

"You call me as soon as you know something, you hear me?"

"I will, Penny," I said. "I promise."

I hung up and looked at Jerry.

"We goin' ta L.A.?"

I rubbed my face.

"We'd have to get our plane tickets pretty quick—"

"How long would it take to drive?" he asked.

"Drive?"

"Yeah," Jerry said. "By the time we buy tickets, get to the airport, get on a plane—"

"It's only about two hundred and fifty miles," I told him.

"Hell, in your Caddy? We can do that in under three hours."

"Okay," I said. "Let's find the name of the motel where Danny was staying. Then we'll pack the car and head right out."

We started searching for the information we needed. I was hoping we wouldn't have to call Penny again. Finally, we found the motel name and address on her desk calendar.

We drove to my house so I could pack, then went to the Sands to get Jerry's suitcase. After that we went down to the parking lot and tossed the bags in the back of the car.

"I get to drive, right?"

I nodded.

"You get to drive, big guy."

Nineteen

THE DRIVE TO L.A. took less than three hours. Jerry kept the Caddy between ninety and a hundred miles an hour most of the way and, surprisingly, we never got pulled over.

As we entered L.A., Jerry asked, "Where to?"

"Wait," I said. "I've got to wait for my stomach to catch up."

"Aw, Mr. G. . . ."

"I've got directions to the motel Danny was stayin' at," I said. "I want to check there first."

"Sure, Mr. G."

The motel Danny had stayed in was just off 405, about half an hour's drive from Marilyn's house. He might have gotten something closer, but I knew he looked with a budget in mind. After all, I was going to be footing the bill.

We pulled into the parking lot of the Starshine Motor Court.

"You stay in the car," I said. "I want to do this without being noticed, if I can."

"Okay," he said. "I'll watch yer back from here."

I decided to go to the room first. I opened the gate and entered the pool area, taking the stairs to the second level. Penny had written the room number down along with the address. When I got to Danny's room I knocked. I thought, Wouldn't it be a kick if he answered? Well, I was going to have to get my kicks somewhere else. He didn't answer and the door was locked.

I heard something squeaking, turned my head and saw a maid pushing her cart. She wasn't stopping at any of the rooms, so she must have finished for the day—at least, on this floor.

I started fishing around in my pocket, as if looking for my key. I didn't know if this would work. In fact, it probably wouldn't have worked on the maids in the Sands, but maybe here . . . then again, maids in L.A. hotels and motels had probably seen everything.

"Can you help me?" I asked, as she reached me.

She looked at me with bored, middle-aged eyes. Yeah, she'd seen it all. "You want in?"

"I forgot my key—"

"Don't try to bullshit me, mister," she said. "I been pushing this cart for too many years."

"Well . . . okay. See, it's my brother's room and he said—"

"Ten bucks," she said, cutting me off.

"What?"

"Ten bucks and I'll let ya in."

"Okay," I agreed, handing over a sawbuck.

She used her key to open the door, swinging it wide and stepping back.

"Actually," I said, trying one more time, "I think my wife's cheating and using this motel—"

"Yeah, yeah," she said, waving her hand, "you don't say nothin' and I won't say nothin'."

She moved on. I went inside and closed the door behind me. She had obviously already cleaned the room. The bed was neatly made. There were fresh, dry towels in the bathroom. The bottom of the tub was dry. Maybe she hadn't needed to replace the towels.

I looked through the dresser drawers and found nothing. There was no suitcase in the room. Danny may not have had time to pack anything. If he'd followed Marilyn from Tahoe he might have been resourceful enough to get on her flight and follow her all the way. He could have picked up whatever he needed in LAX when they landed, maybe even a t-shirt or two and some underwear. I looked in the wastebasket to see if there were any clothing tags or empty bags, but there was nothing. The maid had done her job well.

In fact, there was nothing in the room to indicate that Danny had ever been there. I went back into the bathroom and looked on the counter. Okay, there was a comb, and a bottle of cologne. It was Hai Karate. Danny used it, but so did a lot of other guys.

Playing detective in the room had gotten me nowhere. I decided to go to the front desk and ask. After all, what was I trying to hide? I just wanted to know if my friend had ever checked in.

I left the room, letting the door lock behind me.

"Sure," the desk clerk said, "he took a room here. Been here . . . what? Four days?"

Sounded right. I had been in Brooklyn for three days. The desk clerk had answered my question for the same price it took to get the maid to open the door. I wasn't sure if I had gotten a deal or not.

"Have you seen him lately?"

"Whataya mean lately?"

The clerk was in his fifties, and had been dozing when I walked in. I had the feeling he spent a lot of his time dozing.

"Today? Yesterday? Maybe you saw him comin' in, goin' out?"

"Nope."

"You sure?"

"I hear and see everything."

"You didn't hear or see me come in."

He showed me a wolfish, yellow-toothed grin. "Yeah, I did."

"Okay," I said, "okay."

"If he came in late or early, then I wouldn't've been here. You'd have to talk to whoever was on nights."

"And who would that be?"

"Mmm, that'd be . . . Harry two nights, and . . . oh, yeah, Hilary the other two." From the guy's tone of voice Hilary was apparently a babe.

"What time do they come on?"

"Whoever it is tonight would be comin' on at eleven tonight. Leaves at 7:00 A.M. You'll catch 'em any time between there."

"Okay, thanks."

"Don't let 'em hit ya for more than a sawbuck. It ain't worth more."

"Oh, yeah, thanks."

I started out, stopped at the door and turned back.

"Where would I go to talk to the police who handle this area?"

"That'd be the West Los Angeles Station. You want directions?"

"How much will it cost me?"

He made a face and said, "Up to you. I trust ya to do the right thing."

He wrote the directions down for me.

I gave him a fin.

Twenty

MARILYN'S NEW HOUSE WAS in Brentwood, which was very high-end. We got off 405 at Wilshire Boulevard, which became West San Vicente Boulevard, and took that to South Carmelina Avenue. That took us to Marilyn's street, 12305 Fifth Helena Drive. When we got there Jerry parked in front and turned off the engine.

"Now what?" he asked. "We go in?"

"We should've called first," I said. "We're liable to scare her."

"If she's even there," he said. "Maybe she's makin' a movie."

"Let me go in alone, first," I said.

"Aw, Mr. G. . . ."

"I just don't want to scare her, Jerry," I said. "Once I'm in and see that she's fine, I'll call you in."

"Really?"

"Yes," I said, getting out of the car, "I promise."

All the streets running off of Carmelina were known as the "Numbered Helenas." They were all dead ends. Marilyn's house was a Spanish hacienda-style with a red-tiled roof, white stucco walls, and casement windows. There was also a pool, and small guesthouse. The gate, given Marilyn's state of mind, was oddly open. I walked up the drive to the house, which looked kind of small by Hollywood standards.

I approached the big arched doorway, and rang the bell. There was a small window in the door, only good for peering out. I saw blond hair, then a blurry face. I thought the dense glass had made the face blurry until she opened the door a crack. Okay, her face wasn't blurry, but her eyes were.

"Eddie?"

"Yes, it's me, Marilyn. Eddie."

She swung the door open and threw herself into my arms. My arms were filled with lush, soft female and my body reacted. I was embarrassed—which was new for me. I didn't want her to think that all I wanted was what every other man wanted. I pushed her away, held her by her shoulders, and made like I was looking her over. She was wearing jeans and a sweatshirt, no shoes.

"Are you all right?" I asked.

"I—yes," she said, touching her hair, "I suppose so." She had no lipstick on, and I was so used to seeing those bloodred lips that they looked paler than pale. The bottom one also looked as if she had been biting it.

"Come in, Eddie, come in." She grabbed my wrists and started to pull me in.

"Marilyn, somebody's with me. Can I bring him in?"

"W-who is it?"

"It's a friend of mine—a big guy named Jerry. He's sort of like a bodyguard."

"For me?" Her eyes went wide.

"Well, actually for me. Look, he's harmless, nice . . . and he's a real fan."

"Eddie . . . I look awful."

"You look great."

And she did. Even pale and trembling she oozed sex. She couldn't help it.

"You bring him in," she said. "I'm gonna touch up."

"Marilyn—" But she ran inside.

I went back down the walk and waved to Eddie, signaling him to bring the car up the drive. When he got past the gate I made him stop so no other car could get by.

"That gate should be closed, Mr. G."

"When we get inside we'll find out how to close it. Come on."

He stopped moving.

"Inside?"

"That's right."

"Marilyn's house?"

"Yeah."

"B-but . . . is she home?"

"Yeah, she's home," I said. "Come on, the front door's open and I wanna go in."

"Mr. G.," he said, "we been drivin' a long time."

"You can freshen up inside, Jerry," he said. I suddenly became aware that I was kind of rank myself. "We both can."

I led him through the front door. It was a small, one-story house with an attached garage and a cathedral ceiling.

"Wow," Eddie said.

I assumed Marilyn was still in her bedroom, so I found the bathroom and Jerry and I took turns cleaning up. Eventually, we were both back in the living room, waiting for Marilyn.

"What do I say when she comes out?" Jerry asked.

"Try hello, big guy."

It took several more minutes but Marilyn finally breezed into the room. Her red mouth was lushly in place, her hair combed and gleaming. She was still wearing jeans and the sweatshirt, but the shirt had artfully slid off one rounded, pale shoulder. She was once again the Marilyn of every man and boy's wet dream. For me she was Sugar Kane Kowalczyk of *Some Like It Hot*.

"Marilyn, this is my friend, Jerry."

Jerry opened his mouth but nothing came out. He was staring. I'd never seen the big guy so dumbstruck.

Twenty-one

HELLO, JERRY," MARILYN SAID pleasantly. She walked up to him and put out her hand. Jerry still didn't say a word, but he shook her hand, engulfing it in his.

"Eddie told me you're a big fan."

"Uhh, yes, ma'am."

"I'm always so happy to meet a real fan."

"Oh, I'm a real fan, ma'am," Jerry assured her. "I loved you as Kay in *River of No Return* and as Cherie in *Bus Stop*."

"*Bus Stop*," she said. "That was hard. I got bronchitis during the filming, but I did perfect that Texas-Oklahoma twang."

"You sure did," Jerry said. "That was a great performance."

"*River of No Return* was a bad movie," she said, "but I loved working with Robert Mitchum."

"It may not have been a good movie," Jerry said, "but it's one of my favorites."

"You're sweet," she said, and then looked at me. "I like him."

"That's good," I said, "because he's gonna be around for a while."

"He is?"

"I am?" Jerry asked.

"Before we get to that, Marilyn, do you know a man named Danny Bardini?"

She frowned, putting a pretty little wrinkle in the smooth skin of her forehead.

"No, I don't. Should I?"

"He's a friend of mine, a private eye," I said. "He was keepin' an eye on you for me."

"Following me?"

"Only from Tahoe to here," I said.

"I thought you were going to help me," she said, "not some friend of yours."

"Mr. G. had to go to a funeral," Jerry said, before I could say a word. "His mother died."

"Oh, Eddie." She put her hand on my arm. "I'm sorry."

"It's all right," I said. "I only had Danny watching you until I got back."

"Well, he never came up to me," she said.

"Did you feel someone was watching you these past few days?" I asked.

"Well, I did . . . maybe it was him?"

"Maybe," I said. "Or maybe he saw who was watching you."

"Can you ask him?"

"That's just it," I said. "He's missing."

"Missing?" she asked. "W-what does it mean?"

"It means I think Jerry should stay in your guesthouse until I find out what's going on."

"What about you?" Jerry asked. "You need me to watch your back."

"Jerry, right now I think I need you to watch out for Marilyn," I said. "If somethin' happened to Danny—"

"Can't you stay, Eddie?" Marilyn asked, grabbing my arm.

"I'll come back," I promised. "It may take me a few days to

find Danny, but I'll come back each night. Meanwhile, Jerry will stay with you. Are you working right now?"

"No, we're still having some problems with that script, so I'm just . . . staying around here."

And drinking, I thought, maybe worse. I'd have to have Jerry keep an extra-careful eye on her.

"Can't Jerry look for your friend?"

"No," I said, "he's my friend, my responsibility. I sent him here. If anything's happened to him it's my fault."

Marilyn looked from me to Jerry and dropped her hand from my arm.

"All right, Eddie," she said, in a little girl's voice. "Whatever you say."

"Jerry, let's get your suitcase from the car."

"Okay, Mr. G."

It wasn't a two-man job, but he knew I wanted to talk to him outside.

At the car I said, "I'm gonna go and talk to the local cops."

"And you don't want me along?"

"I know you don't think the cops do any good, Jerry, but I've got to find out if anything happened to Danny. He could be in jail, or . . ."

"Or the morgue."

"Right."

"Okay, Mr. G.," he said, "but you call if you need me."

"Let's go back inside. I'll take down Marilyn's number, and we'll see if the guesthouse has a phone. Also, you can take a look around the grounds, see if it looks like anyone's been here."

"Okay, Mr. G."

"Jerry," I asked, "didn't we talk about you callin' me Eddie?"

"Yeah, Mr. G.," he said, "we talked about it."

Twenty-two

I PRESENTED MYSELF at the West Los Angeles Station of the L.A. Police Department.

"You want to talk to a detective?" the desk sergeant asked. His name tag said his name was Clemmons.

"That's right."

"Do you want to report a crime?"

"Not a crime, exactly."

"Then what?"

"Well . . . maybe a missing person."

"Who's missin'?"

"A friend of mine."

"We only take missing persons reports from family members," the sergeant said. "Are you a family member?"

"Uh, I—look, I just need to talk to som—"

"Can you produce a family member?"

"I—no, look—um, I'm the closest thing to a family member."

"What's your relation?"

"Cousin—second cousin."

He stared at me.

"Is that not close enough? Should I have just stuck with cousin?"

"Sir—"

"Can I give you his name and find out if he's been arrested? Hospitalized? Killed?"

"You think he might've been killed?"

"I hope not. Look, I can't find him, I'm just tryin' to decide how worried to get. If you guys have him in a cell, I'd prefer that to the morgue."

"Can't say I blame you," Sergeant Clemmons said. "Let me have his name, your name and I'll check. Have a seat."

I sat for half an hour when a tall, dark-haired, very slender man wearing a suit approached me. I stood up slowly, not liking the look on his face.

"Mr. Gianelli?"

"That's right."

"I'm Detective Robert Stanze. I understand you're looking for a man named Daniel Bardini?"

"That's right. Have you—" I almost said "found him," but the words stuck in my throat.

"We have two unidentified males in our morgue," he said.

"T-two?"

"Well, we have more than that," Stanze said, "but two match the description of your—of Daniel Bardini. At least, the description you've given us."

"I see."

"Would you be willing to take a look and see if . . . ?"

I felt my eyes burning, the foyer we were standing in closed in on me.

"Sir, are you all right?"

"I—" I cleared my throat. "I am, yes. And yes, I'll take a look."

"Come with me, please."

The morgue was cold. I had been to a morgue in Vegas once. It hadn't felt this cold.

Two bodies, covered by sheets on separate tables.

"Ready?" Stanze asked.

"Is anybody ever ready for this?"

"No, sir."

"Okay," I said, "then I'm ready."

The attendant grasped the sheet on the first body and rolled it down to the dead man's waist.

"No," I said, "that's not him."

"Good," Stanze said.

I guess we were both glad I had been able to dodge that bullet. The attendant covered the poor guy up and we moved to the next table. True to my Vegas background I was wondering what the odds were that man number two was Danny Bardini.

We positioned ourselves at the table, Stanze and me on one side, the attendant on the other.

"Ready for this one?" Stanze asked.

I thought he was incredibly sensitive for a detective. The Vegas dicks I'd dealt with wouldn't have cared if I was ready or not. In fact, I knew one who would have taken real pleasure in peeling the sheet down and showing me Danny's body.

I felt nauseous.

"Mr. Gianelli?"

I was afraid if I opened my mouth I'd vomit, so instead I just nodded.

"Okay," Stanze said to the attendant.

The man nodded, grasped the top of the sheet and pulled it down.

Twenty-three

DETECTIVE STANZE TOOK ME into an office.

"This is my lieutenant's office, but he's not in today," he said, seating himself behind the man's desk. He looked uncomfortable.

"Okay, neither body was that of your, uh, cousin, Danny Bardini," he said, sitting back in the chair. It slipped and he righted himself before he could fall. Further proof that he wasn't used to sitting there. "You want to tell me about him and what he was doing when he went missing?"

I had been giving this some thought ever since I saw the face of the second dead man and realized it wasn't Danny. How much to tell the detective? And then I thought, why not tell him everything—except about Jerry.

"Okay," I said, "I work in Las Vegas at the Sands Hotel and Casino. I'm a pit boss there, but sometimes I'm called on to do special favors for our celebrity customers."

"You mean like get them tickets to shows, or girls? Like that?"

"Not quite."

"Go on."

"You can check this out with a simple phone call to my boss, Jack Entratter," I said. "I can give you the phone number—"

"If I want to check it out I won't call any number you give me, Mr. Gianelli," he said, cutting me off. "I can look up the number for the Sands and call myself. But for now, why don't you just continue with your story?"

"I was asked by Dean Martin to try to help a friend of his who was having some trouble."

"What friend?"

I hesitated, then said, "Marilyn Monroe."

"Dean Martin and Marilyn Monroe," he repeated.

"That's right."

He stared at me for a moment, then said, "Okay, go on."

I told him how Marilyn felt she was being watched and followed. How I'd asked Danny to keep an eye on her, and then was called away to New York for a funeral. In my absence Danny had followed Marilyn all the way home to make sure she was all right.

"He called his secretary, told her what motel he was staying in, and now he's missing and she hasn't been able to locate him."

"Have you gone to his motel?"

"Yes."

"And he wasn't there?"

"No," I said, "but I talked with the desk clerk and he did check in."

"And when did the clerk see him last?"

"When he checked in," I said. "He suggested the night man or girl might have seen him later. I was going to go back later and ask."

"Where are you staying?" he asked. "At that same motel?"

I hadn't gotten myself a room anywhere.

"At Miss Monroe's."

"In her house?"

"No, she has a guesthouse."

He drummed his fingers on the desktop.

"Detective, why would I lie about things that can be checked out?"

"Okay," he said, "sit here a while. Don't get impatient. I'll be back."

"I'll be here."

He left. I knew he was going to check up on me, I just didn't know how much checking he was going to do. I tried to follow his advice, but it was easier said than done.

Detective Stanze returned in half an hour.

"Okay," he said, "let's go."

"Where?"

"Out to the Starshine Motor Court."

"Did you check—"

"I called the Sands Hotel," he said. "It's only because that checked out that we're driving out to the motel to check on the rest of it. Come on, you and me. Let's go."

In the hallway I said, "I have my car."

"Good," Stanze said. "I'll follow you."

"Just the two of us?"

"That's what I said, pal," he replied. "Just you and me."

Apparently, he wasn't going to assign any other men to the job until he knew for sure what the hell was going on.

I was hoping we'd both know that pretty damn soon.

Twenty-four

WHEN WE ARRIVED AT the motel I pulled up in front. Stanze parked his unmarked car behind me. We went inside and found the same clerk behind the desk.

"Hey," I said.

He looked at me and asked, "Can I help you?"

"I'm Detective Stanze, LAPD," Stanze said, showing his badge. "Do you know this gentleman?"

The clerk looked at me and said, "Nope. Should I?"

"You should," I said. "I talked to you this morning about one of your guests. Danny Bardini?"

"You talked to me?" he asked. "Come on, pal, how much did you have to drink last night?"

Stanze looked at me.

"What are you tryin' to pull?" I demanded. "We talked about my buddy, Danny Bardini. He was staying in room two-one-five."

"Two-one-five?"

"Would you check and see if you have anyone by that name in room two-one-five?" Stanze asked.

"Sure thing." The clerk checked his register, then shook his head. "That room's empty."

"When was it last occupied?"

"About two days ago."

"By a Danny Bardini?"

"Nope," the clerk said. "A woman."

"What the hell—" I said.

Stanze put his hand on my arm.

"No."

"What is your name?" he asked the clerk.

"Max."

"Well, Max, I'd like to see room two-one-five."

"I'll take you up there," the clerk said. "Do I gotta take him, too?"

"Just give me your key."

"I don't think I can—"

"Come on, Max," Stanze said. "I don't have all day. *Comprende*?"

Max shrugged and said, "Okay, okay."

He turned to grab his passkey, looked around, seemed lost for a minute, then found it and handed it over.

"Somebody's always movin' it, the damn thing."

"Thanks."

Stanze and I left the office and walked up a flight. He unlocked the door and we went in.

"Clean," he said.

"It was clean when I came in," I said.

"The clerk let you in here?"

"No, one of the maids."

"And it was like this?"

"Yeah," I said, "like she had just finished, except . . ."

I went into the bathroom. The counter was cleared off.

"There was a toothbrush and a bottle of Hai Karate here." I sniffed the air. "You can still smell it."

He sniffed.

"Lots of people wear Hai Karate."

"Do you?"

"No."

"Your partner."

"No."

"You work with anybody who does?"

He thought a moment, then said, "Okay, I get it."

"The towels were dry, and so was the bottom of the tub. Danny takes a shower every day, so he wasn't in here last night."

"No luggage?"

"He might not have had any," I said. "He was following Marilyn, so he didn't have much time to pack. He would have picked stuff up when he landed."

"Like a toothbrush and cologne."

"Right."

Stanze nodded, put his hands on his hips and looked around.

"Okay, let's go."

"Wait," I said, "that clerk is lying, Detective."

"I know."

"You . . . you what?"

"I know he's lying," he said. "I've been a detective for more than five minutes, Mr. Gianelli. I saw how he didn't know where the key was. And if he was a longtime desk clerk he would've come up here and let us in. He never would've given up the key that easily."

"Really? You think clerks are that efficient?"

"This is a hot sheet motel," he said. "The last thing they want is a cop snooping around on his own."

"Then you do believe me," I said with relief.

"I believe something is going on."

"So you'll take that guy Max in?"

"No," Stanze said. "You and me are going to make him think

that I believe him and not you, and then I'm going to watch him and this place. I also want to talk to Miss Monroe."

"That's not a problem."

"Good. Then let's go downstairs and put on a show for our friend."

Twenty-five

WE PULLED UP IN Marilyn's driveway. Stanze allowed me to go in first and prepare her. He had heard that she was "fragile."

I went to the door and rang the bell.

"Eddie—" she said when she opened it, but I grabbed her shoulders, pushed her inside and closed the door behind us.

"Marilyn, where's Jerry?"

"He's in the kitchen," she said, eyes wide. "He made me these fantastic grilled cheese sandwiches. He's a great cook—"

"Let's go in the kitchen."

"What's wrong?"

"Tell you in a minute."

"Hey, Mr. G.," Jerry said when we walked in. "You want something to eat?"

"No, Jerry. Listen up. I've got a cop outside. A detective. I checked with the LAPD and they have no record of arresting Danny. Also, he's not in the morgue. This detective is being very helpful, and he believes what I'm tellin' him."

"Why wouldn't he, Mr. G.?"

"I'll tell you later," I said. "Right now I think you should go out the back to the guesthouse and stay there. We'll keep you being here to ourselves, as insurance."

The doorbell rang.

"We need insurance, Mr. G.?" Jerry asked.

"We might, Jerry. Somethin's goin' on. I'll tell you about it later."

"Okay, Mr. G., whatever you say."

Jerry went out the back door.

"Should I let the detective in, Eddie?" Marilyn asked.

"I'll get it, Marilyn," I said. "Listen, you can tell this man the truth, just don't mention Jerry, okay?"

"I understand, Eddie. How do I look?"

"Like a dream."

"Oh, Eddie . . ."

I went to answer the door.

Stanze didn't want it to show, but Marilyn had the same effect on him that she had on all men, especially in person.

"Miss Monroe, I just need to verify a few things that Mr. Gianelli has told me, and then ask you a few other questions. All right?"

"Okay."

He looked at me. "No offense, but I'd like to do this alone."

He didn't want me coaching her.

"No problem. I'll wait in the kitchen. You, uh, want a grilled cheese sandwich, Detective?"

"No, thanks."

I went into the kitchen. The sandwiches had cooled off, but they were still good.

Marilyn told me later how the interview had gone down . . .

"Mr. Gianelli tells me he met you through Dean Martin. Is that true?"

"Yes, it is."

"You're friends with Mr. Martin?"

"Yes."

"Ma'am, I really don't mean to offend you, but—"

"Dino and I are just friends, Detective," she said. "I do have men in my life who are just friends."

"Like Eddie?"

"Yes," she said, "exactly like Eddie."

"Okay," he said.

They went over Marilyn's problem about her feeling she was being watched. Also, the way she felt about being blamed for Clark Gable's death.

"Well, that's just silly," Stanze said. "I read about him doing his own stunts. He was too old to be doing that stuff."

"I know," she said. "We tried to tell him . . ."

"We?"

"Me and Kay, his wife."

"I see. Now, Mr. Gianelli tells me you never saw his friend? Danny?"

"No, sir. I guess he was very good at his job."

"Um, yeah . . . have you seen anyone watching your house lately?"

"No."

"Following you?"

"I haven't been out in days."

"Why not?"

She shrugged. "I guess I don't want to be followed."

"So you feel if you go out someone will follow you?"

"Yes."

"And you don't mean, like, photographers?"

"Oh, no. They're always there. No, I mean . . . someone else."

"Like who?"

She shrugged again. "I don't know. Just somebody."

"Miss Monroe, what is Eddie Gianelli supposed to do for you?"

"Protect me," she said. "Make me feel better."

"Why would Dean Martin ask him to do that for you?"

"He and Dino are good friends," she said. "And Dino, if he came around me, that would just attract more attention. Do you see? And people would get the wrong idea. Like they always do."

"I see," he said. "I do." He closed his notebook. "Ma'am, do you want to make a report about being followed?"

"Oh, no."

"Why not?"

"The studio wouldn't like it. I'm supposed to start a shoot soon, and they wouldn't like the publicity."

"Ma'am, there's a man missing, and you could probably use some protection."

"Oh, but I have—" She stopped short, realizing she'd almost said she had "Eddie and Jerry."

"You have what?"

"I have Eddie."

Stanze had a few more words for me after questioning Marilyn.

"Look," he'd said, "I know something's going on, I just don't know what. I'd like to believe you don't know what, either, and that you're not keeping anything from me."

"We've told you everything."

"No offense," he said, "but it's my experience that no one tells the cops everything."

He started to leave, but had one more question.

"Tell me, why did you have your friend Danny tail Marilyn instead of introducing him and having him travel with her, stay at her house with her?"

"The truth?"

"That would be refreshing for a cop."

"Danny's my best friend, but he's a dog with women. I didn't want to expose Marilyn to him. I didn't want him to be tempted."

"You didn't trust your own friend with Marilyn Monroe?"

"I've never trusted Danny with any woman."

"Okay," he said, "I get it."

He left, telling me he'd be in touch. I told him I'd be in the guesthouse, and we gave him that phone number, which was separate from the main house.

When Jerry came back inside I filled him and Marilyn in about Danny's motel, and how the clerk denied he'd ever spoken to me before.

"What's goin' on, Mr. G.?" Jerry asked. "Why would the clerk tell you he was there, and then tell the cops he never heard of either one of you."

"Whoever's behind this doesn't want the cops to believe anything I say."

"But why?" Marilyn asked. "And what does it have to do with me?"

"Marilyn," I said, "the only thing I think we can be sure of is that it all has something to do with you. It begins and ends with you."

"So . . . what do we do?" she asked.

Jerry looked at me, expecting me to come up with an answer.

"We have to do something," I said, "that nobody would expect."

"Like what?" Jerry asked.

I looked at Marilyn, who was gazing up at me with that Marilyn look, breathing through her mouth.

"We have to take Marilyn away from them."

Twenty-six

JERRY MADE DINNER that night.

The atmosphere in the kitchen was festive. Marilyn got a big kick out of the fact that Jerry had managed to throw together a hot dinner using what little food she had in her cupboards and refrigerator. She laughed with delight like a little girl, and I wondered why her life couldn't be like this every day. Why was there so much sadness and fear in her world when, to the world at large, she seemed to have everything?

But beneath the laughter that night was my concern for Danny and Penny, my confusion about what had happened at the motel.

When Marilyn excused herself to use "the little girl's room" I asked Jerry, "Did you check the grounds today for any sign that somebody's been watching the house?"

"I took a walk around," he said. "I ain't Daniel Boone but I know what a bunch of cigarette butts behind a tree mean."

"So there was someone?"

"The butts seemed fresh," Jerry said. "They haven't been

rained on yet. We could check and see when it rained last, but I'd say somebody's been in the bushes recently."

"Somebody who has the resources to make Danny disappear from a motel."

"According to that one clerk," Jerry said. "Didn't you say you paid a maid to let you in the room?"

"That's right, I did."

"Seems to me that maid might know somethin' more than she let on," Jerry said. "That is, unless she disappeared, too."

"Okay, so I've got to go back to that motel and talk to more employees and the owner. But still, that leaves us asking who these people are who got the clerk to lie?"

"Whoever they are they had to spread a lot of money around that place," Jerry said. "But since you don't have as much money to spread, you need me to make the difference."

"You have to stay with Marilyn."

"I gotta stay with you, Mr. G.," Jerry argued. "We can find someplace to stash Marilyn where she'll be safe. Like you said before, we gotta take her away, put her where they can't find her."

"That still doesn't tell us who *they* are, or what they did with Danny."

"Once they can't find her," Jerry said, "they'll come after you."

"You know," I said, "she's been connected to so many people—Johnny Roselli, the Kennedys—"

"Joe DiMaggio," Jerry said.

"Well, she was married to him, and just recently divorced Arthur Miller."

"Joe DiMaggio wouldn't have nothin' ta do with this," Jerry said with finality. "Maybe that Miller guy is havin' her watched because he's still in love with her."

But I was thinking about the Kennedy family. Old Joe had

suffered a heart attack the year before, right after I'd talked with him at a house in Tahoe. Even though he'd survived, it had put him in a wheelchair, from which he was still running the Kennedy clan.

He never approved of Jack's friendship with Frank, certainly didn't approve of his son, the president, having show business friends. Did Joe know about Jack and Marilyn? Did he know about Bobby and Marilyn? Was any of this gossip true?

And if it was, to what lengths would Joe go to keep them apart? Would he use the Secret Service, as he had done last year when I was trying to help Sammy? Or would he use the FBI? No, Hoover would never allow that. Hoover hated the Kennedys.

So to what length would Hoover go to discredit the Kennedys?

Hoover and the Secret Service. They'd have plenty of money to spread around. And they would certainly have a lot more than just money.

"So where are we gonna take her—" Jerry started, but I shushed him.

"What—" he started, then got it when I pointed to my ear.

"Any more of that casserole left?" Marilyn asked, coming back into the kitchen.

"Sure is, Miss Monroe."

"Jerry, sweetie," she said, "I asked you to call me Marilyn."

"I know, Miss Monroe, but . . . I just can't."

He spooned the last of his tuna casserole onto a plate and put it in front of her.

"I know!" she said excitedly. "Could you do for me the same thing you do with Eddie?"

Jerry looked confused.

"Could you call me Miss M.?"

"Sure thing, Miss M.," he said. "I can do that."

✳   ✳   ✳

We all watched TV together until Marilyn announced she was going to bed. She came around and kissed us both good night on the cheek before she went. She smelled so damned good.

"Night, Eddie," she said. "Night, sweetie."

"Night Miss M.," Jerry said.

I wondered when Jerry had become "sweetie" while I was still "Eddie."

"I think I hate you, Mr. G.," Jerry said from his supine position on Marilyn Monroe's sofa.

"Why?"

"I used ta think Marilyn Monroe was the sexiest doll in the world."

"And now?"

"Now? She's like my little sister. I hate you for that."

"I know what you mean," I said. "I hate Dean Martin for the same reason."

"Aw, ya can't hate Dino."

"And you," I said, "can't hate me. I guess we better turn in, too. Is there a sofa in the guesthouse?"

"Yeah, but you can have the bed."

"That's okay," I said. "I'll take the sofa. I'm smaller."

"Yeah, you are."

I stood up and beckoned him to follow me. We went to the front door and stepped outside.

"What are ya thinkin', Mr. G.?" he asked, going right back to our conversation in the kitchen.

"The Kennedys," I said. "The Secret Service. Hoover. The FBI?"

He stared at me, and then suddenly a light dawned. "You think somebody might have her house bugged?" he asked, lowering his voice.

"Could be," I said. "Just in case, I don't want to discuss plans inside."

"What about the guesthouse?"

"Might be bugged, too. Let's just talk out here."

"Okay, we could put her in a hotel."

"Somebody might recognize her."

"She could stay with a friend."

"I get the feeling that's not an option."

"Well, who does she trust?" Jerry asked.

"Dino . . . I guess."

"Where does he live?"

"Beverly Hills," I said, "but we don't know if he's home."

"What about Mr. S.?" Jerry asked.

I stared at him. "That's a damned good idea," I said. "He lives in Palm Springs, and he's home because he's getting the house ready for Jack Kennedy's visit."

"Do we want Miss M. to be there with JFK?" Jerry asked.

"No," I said, "we'll get her out before he arrives. We just need Frank to keep her safe for a few days."

"Well, he's got George," Jerry said, "and he uses enough bodyguards to keep an army safe."

"We'll need to call him first," I said.

"He'll say yes."

"We still need to call him, but not from here."

"I got his number," Jerry said. "We can head for Palm Springs and call him on the way."

"Okay," I said, "we'll get Marilyn up early and head out."

"How far is Palm Springs?"

"About a hundred miles, give or take."

"In your car we'll be there and back in a snap. And then we can check out the motel."

"Good. Now why don't you turn in?"

"I'm gonna take a walk around the grounds first," he said.

"And just to be safe," I said, "I'll sleep on Marilyn's couch instead of the one in the guesthouse."

"Why don't we all just sleep in the house?" he asked.

"That's a good idea," I said. "We've already had an unexplained disappearance. Why chance any more?"

"Or we can all disappear at the same time."

"I could have done without hearing that, Jerry."

"Sorry, Mr. G."

He turned to leave and I grabbed his arm.

"Forget about checking the grounds. Let's go back inside. We've got to stay together."

"But if they're watchin'—"

"Let 'em watch," I said. "Let's get some shut-eye."

"Okay."

As we turned to go in I said, "You've got your gun, right?"

He patted his chest and said, "Right here, Mr. G. Right here."

Twenty-seven

IN THE MORNING WE GOT Jerry's suitcase from the guesthouse and mine from the car. Marilyn objected to being woken up so early. She was definitely not a morning person, which was probably why she had a reputation for being late to the set.

"Where are we going so early?" she kept demanding.

"We'll tell you later," I said. "Let's just get going."

"I have to shower," she said, "and do my makeup and hair."

"Okay, but make it quick."

She smiled at me and asked, "Have you met me?"

"Uh—"

She pushed me. "Get out now, and let me get ready."

I got out of her bedroom and went to the kitchen where Jerry had made coffee.

"Thought we'd have breakfast out," he said, "but this'll get us started."

We sat at the table, had a cup each, and then another, while we waited, like many directors and costars and crew had waited in the past, for Marilyn Monroe.

✳ ✳ ✳

After we got on 10 we told Marilyn where we were going and why.

"So you really do think I'm in danger?" she asked.

"Don't sound so relieved," I said.

"It's just . . . nobody has ever believed me before," she said. "I mean . . . not about much of anything. Especially not when I say I'm sick, or that I'm being watched, or followed. Nothing." When she said "nothing" she shrugged her shoulders and her voice went way up at the end, almost like Betty Boop's.

Marilyn was in the back and I was turned in the passenger seat so I could talk to her. The wind was blowing her hair, but she told us not to put the top up.

"Does Frank know we're coming?" she asked.

"Not yet," I said. "We're gonna stop along the way and call. If he tells us not to come—"

"He won't," she said.

She seemed positive, even though their relationship had ended some time ago and Frank had since moved on to Juliet Prowse.

"I'm gonna pull up at this service station for gas," Jerry said. "You can use the phone here."

"Good."

"I can call him," Marilyn said.

"No," I said, "I'll do it." I thought having her call would be pushing it.

While I went to the phone Marilyn stayed in the backseat and Jerry stood outside the car, leaning against it with his arms folded. He never took his eyes off the highway. He wanted to see if we were being followed. I promised Marilyn I'd bring her a Coke.

George Jacobs answered on the fourth ring. He had been Frank's "man" for many years. We'd met but I didn't know if he'd remember.

"George, this is Eddie Gianelli. I, uh, work at the Sands—"

"I know who you are, Mr. Gianelli," he said. "What can I do for you?"

"I need to talk to Frank."

"What is it about?"

"Marilyn Monroe."

"Mr. Gianelli, Mr. Sinatra ended that romantic entanglement—"

"This isn't about romance," I said. "It's about life and death." A little dramatic, maybe, but I thought it would do the trick.

"Please wait," George said.

I waited. After a few minutes Frank came on the line.

"Hey, Eddie! Sorry, man, I'm supervising the construction, ya know? For Jack's visit? Hey, where are ya?"

"On 10, halfway between L.A. and Palm Springs, Frank. I've got Marilyn and Jerry with me."

"Jerry? Lewis?"

"Epstein."

"Oh, Big Jerry. Yeah, George told me you said something about Marilyn. You know, Eddie, bringin' her here, that's gonna be uncomfortable . . ."

"I would've taken her to Dino's, but I don't think he's home, and Jeannie, she probably wouldn't—"

"What's goin' on, Eddie?"

I told Frank that Marilyn was bring watched—we had proof of that—and that Danny had disappeared.

"And this has something to do with Marilyn?"

"It *has* to."

"So she really is being watched?"

"And probably followed."

"The poor kid," Frank said. "Yeah, Eddie, bring her here. By all means. I hope the noise doesn't bother her but, yeah, I'll have George get a room ready for her."

"Okay, Frank. Thanks."

"You and Jerry, you'll stay for some spaghetti?" he asked hopefully. Frank really liked playing the role of host.

My first instinct was to say no, we had to turn right around and go back, but I knew Jerry would kill me.

"Sure, Frank. Sounds good. Thanks."

"See ya soon, Eddie."

When I got back to the car I handed Marilyn her bottle of Coke and went to stand by Jerry.

"Whataya think?"

"I don't see nobody," Jerry said. "Didn't see nobody in the rearview mirror, either."

"You think we got away from L.A. without bein' followed?" I asked.

"Either that," Jerry said, "or they're really, really good at it. What did Mr. S. say?"

"He said bring her."

"I told you he would," Marilyn said, drinking from the straw stuck in the bottle.

I looked at her. "We should be there in about half an hour. Frank said he hoped the construction won't bother you."

"It won't."

"You get gas?" I asked Jerry.

"All done."

"Let's go, then."

We got back into the car.

"You didn't want a Coke, did you?" I asked Jerry.

"No."

He started the car and I turned in my seat to see if any of the customers at the pumps were paying us any attention.

"Is everything all right, Eddie?" Marilyn asked, putting her hand on my shoulder. There was a look of concern on her face that I wanted to wipe away. Sometimes, when she looked at me with those eyes, that was all I wanted to do.

"So far," I said, patting her hand, "everything's fine."

But Jerry was right about one thing. Suddenly Marilyn was like a kid sister.

I hated me, too.

Twenty-eight

FRANK WAS SPENDING THOUSANDS. He was building an additional wing of guest suites, installing extra telephones and—as Dean had told me earlier—had put in a helipad. Somehow Frank had gotten it into his head that his house would become the Western White House.

As we turned into the drive an expensive red sports car coming the other way almost hit us. Only Jerry's reflexes avoided the collision. I saw a woman driving, thought I recognized her.

We drove up through the construction and saw George waving to us. Jerry pulled up right in front of George, who made a stopping gesture with both hands. Then he ran over and opened the back door for Marilyn.

"Hello, Miss Monroe. Welcome back." He spoke loudly because of the jackhammering that was going on. The air was thick with dust.

"Hello, Georgie," she said, kissing him on the cheek.

I guess I should have figured that she'd been there before, but this was the first time I was sure of it.

"I have a room ready for you," George said. "Your suitcase?"

"In the trunk," she said. "I have three."

And that was only because I wouldn't let her bring two others.

"I'll get the bags," Jerry said.

I hung back so I could carry one. By the time we caught up, Frank was embracing Marilyn rather awkwardly.

"Hey, kid," Frank said, "how ya doin'?"

"I'm okay, Frank."

"George fixed up a room," he said. "Why don't you go and freshen up? Then we'll eat."

"Okay."

"I can take that," George said, grabbing the bag I was holding. He led Marilyn into the house and Jerry followed with the other two bags.

Behind me the hammering suddenly stopped. Up here by the main house the dust wasn't as thick.

"What a mess, huh?" Frank asked. "I had to cover the pool to keep the dust outta the water. Whataya think of the place?"

"It looks great, Frank."

"Come 'ere," he said, pulling me over to the other side of the deck. "See it?"

From there I could see the concrete helipad.

"Impressive. Hey, was that Ava Gardner I saw tearin' out of here in a red sports car?"

"Oh, yeah," he said, rolling his eyes. "Ava was here when you called."

"She looked pretty mad," I said. "She almost hit us. Are you . . . gettin' back together? What happened to Juliet?"

"Juliet is still in the picture," Frank said, "but me and Ava, we're always gonna be in each other's lives. We can't live without each other, but we also can't live together."

"So what was she so mad about?"

"Marilyn," Frank said. "I told her you were bringin' Marilyn. She flipped."

"I didn't know, Frank," I said. "I'm sorry. You should've told me on the phone."

"Don't sweat it, Eddie. The kid needs help and I'm gonna give it to her. Ava'll have to get over it."

"And Juliet?"

He laughed.

"What Juliet don't know won't hurt her. Now, come on. We got spaghetti to eat."

Twenty-nine

MARILYN WATCHED IN AWE as Jerry ate more spaghetti than the three of us combined.

"Oh, my God, Jerry," she said.

He looked up at her puzzled, then sheepish. "I, um, was hungry, Miss M."

"And this was only lunch," she said, looking at Frank, and then me. "What's he going to do for dinner?"

"I'll have to worry about that back in L.A.," I said.

"Do you have to drive right back?" Frank asked. "I have plenty of rooms. You can break in the building."

"JFK's wing?" I asked.

"It's not his until he gets here."

"When is he coming?" Marilyn asked.

"Not for a few weeks," Frank said. "I've got to get all the work done before he comes."

"Well," I said, "we can't stay. We have to find out what happened to Danny."

"Do you need any other help?" Frank asked.

I jerked my head at Frank, signaling him to follow me away from the table, leaving Marilyn to watch Jerry eat.

"Frank, I just need you to keep Marilyn safe. I don't think we were followed, but I don't know who we're dealin' with."

"I've got a couple of bodyguards on full time, Eddie, but I'll add a few more."

"Good. I hope it won't take too long, but—"

"But you really don't know what you're doin'," Frank finished.

"I'm not a detective, Frank, and Jerry, well, he's . . ."

"Jerry."

"Right."

"I've got an idea," he said. "Wait here."

He went off somewhere into the house, came back and handed me a business card.

"Fred Otash?" I asked. "I know that name."

"They call him the Hollywood PI," Frank said.

"Okay, yeah," I said. "I remember now. I heard Dean mention him once."

"He's supposed to be good," Frank said. "I haven't used him, but somebody gave me his card at a party, or something and I threw it in a drawer. I don't remember who gave it to me."

I didn't totally believe that. If he'd tossed it in a drawer when somebody gave it to him, how would he have been able to find it so quickly? But if he didn't want to tell me something, that was his business.

"Okay," I said, "if I decide I need help I'll give him a call."

"And keep in touch. Lemme know what's happening."

"You've got enough going on here, Frank."

"You said it. I just want it to be perfect for Jack, ya know?" he said. "But I do need a distraction once in a while."

I wondered if that was why Ava had been there, as a distraction.

We went back to the table and I said, "Hey, Jerry, you done?"

"Done," he said, then added, "for now. Thanks for the spaghetti, Mr. S."

"Sure thing, Big Jer."

He and Frank headed for the door. I hung back and took Marilyn's hand. We walked to the door slowly.

"You'll be okay here for a while," I said. "It may be awkward with Frank—"

"It's okay, Eddie," she said. "I know Frank is done with me."

"Like I said, it'll only be for a while. But do me a favor, will you?"

"What?"

"Don't call anybody, don't tell anybody where you are."

"Not even my agent?"

"Call your agent once, tell him you're okay and you'll be in touch," I explained. "Don't make any other calls. Not to anyone!"

"You think somebody may be . . . listening?" she asked. "You think Frank's being . . . bugged?"

Actually, I was afraid she was being bugged—her house, her agent—but given Frank's involvement with JFK she might have a point.

"No matter who's listening . . . just don't call anyone, and don't talk to anyone on the phone but me . . . or Jerry."

"Jerry's so sweet."

"Oh, yeah," I said, "he's just a great big teddy bear."

At the door she gave the great big teddy bear a hug and a kiss, then kissed me and whispered in my ear, "Thank you."

Thirty

"WHAT DO YOU THINK about hiring a PI?" I asked Jerry.

"For what?"

"To help find Danny."

We were on Route 111, heading for 10. The ride back to L.A. gave us time to talk about the situation.

"You wanna hire a PI to find a PI?" Jerry asked. "That don't seem outta line."

"No?"

"Mr. G.," he said, "you ain't a PI, and I don't know nothin' about L.A. We need help."

"I'm glad you agree."

"But who you gonna get?"

"Well, if Penny was in Danny's office we'd ask her who he uses here," I said.

"I guess we shoulda looked while we was there."

"Frank gave me a business card for Fred Otash."

"Hey, I know that name."

"Yeah, he's kind of famous out here," I said.

"No," he said, "there's a newspaper in the backseat. I took it from Miss. M.'s place."

I reached back on the seat and brought it up front.

"There's an ad in there, someplace."

I started leafing through the pages and found what he was talking about.

The top line said: "It is important to choose your investigator with as much care as you choose your doctor or lawyer."

"Do we want somebody that famous?" Jerry asked.

I closed the newspaper and tossed it back onto the rear seat.

"We don't know who we're dealin' with, Jerry. Secret Service, FBI, Mafia—"

"You think Mr. Giancana is buggin' Miss M.? Why?" he asked, quick to defend.

"My point is we don't know, Jerry," I said. "What we need is somebody who can find out, somebody connected, and if he happens to be famous I guess we'll have to live with that."

Jerry shrugged. "It's up to you, Mr. G.," he said. "I'm just here to back you up."

"You do more than that, Jerry, believe me."

He took a quick look away from the traffic and at me.

"Thanks, Mr. G."

"Sure."

We drove for a while, then stopped for gas again near West Covina because Jerry didn't like to let the needle go below the halfway point. He said that was the way dirt got into the lines.

While we stood there waiting for the attendant to fill the tank I said, "Let's go back to that motel first. Maybe we'll find that clerk, or the maid, and learn something from them."

"Fine with me," Jerry said. "You find me that clerk and I'll make him talk."

"That I'd like to see, Jerry," I said, "especially after that man looked right through me and lied about ever meeting me."

"We'll get the truth out of him, Mr. G.," Jerry said. "I guarantee it."

I paid for the gas while Jerry got back in the car. When I turned to get in I saw something familiar. After I'd slammed the door Jerry said, "I saw it, too."

"Blue Chrysler?"

"Yeah," he said. "Looks like two men in the front seat. It's been behind us since we got on this highway—what is it, 10?"

"They didn't follow us from L.A.?"

"No."

"Then how the hell did they get onto us comin' back?"

"I don't know," Jerry said. "Maybe at Mr. S.'s?"

"Shit, I hope not," I said. "That means we'll have to go back and get Marilyn."

"Mr. S. has construction guys, bodyguards, and George there all the time," Jerry pointed out. "She'll be safe."

"Yeah, and so far all they've been doin' is watchin' her—whoever *they* are."

"So what do we do?"

I looked at him and said, "Let's find out who these bastards are."

Thirty-one

JERRY MADE SURE THE BLUE CHRYLSER didn't lose us on 10. When we got on to 405 to go to Brentwood I started wondering where we could take those guys.

On San Vicente I told Jerry, "Bypass Marilyn's."

"Where we goin'?"

"To the country club."

"Oh, goody."

The Brentwood Country Club was always busy. The beautiful people needed their recreation. But you couldn't just drive in, you had to stop at the guard's gate and identify yourself. When we pulled in, there were two cars ahead of us. Our tail didn't know where we were going so they turned in to follow. Before they knew it they were in line, a car in front and a car behind.

"Come on," Jerry said.

He was out of the car with his .45 in his fist before I could stop him. I ran after him, hoping that the two guys in the car weren't cops.

Jerry got to the car before they could react. He opened the

driver's side and yanked the guy out, showed the passenger his gun.

"Don't!" he said, in case the second guy was planning to pull a gun.

I got to the passenger side just as the guy put his hands up. I did a quick frisk—as I had seen done plenty of times in the movies—and came up with a gun.

"One here, too," Jerry said, releasing the driver so abruptly he staggered. He tossed the guy's gun into the backseat, so I did the same.

"What the hell is wrong with you guys?" the driver demanded.

The driver behind them leaned on his horn, but when Jerry gave him a look he released it.

"What do you guys want?" I asked. "You been following us at least since Palm Springs, maybe before."

"We don't know what you're talkin' about," the guy in the passenger seat said.

"You got a permit for that rod, bub?" the driver asked Jerry.

"This one sounds like a cop, Mr. G."

"I suggest we get our cars out of the way and have a talk," I said.

"Tell your friend to put the gun away," the driver said. "The security guy's comin' over to see what's goin' on."

"He'll put it away," I said, "but it comes out again if you try to take off."

"Understood. We'll move the car," the driver said, getting back in.

"I'll move the Caddy, Mr. G."

At the same time, the passenger got out. "I'll handle the security guy."

"Right behind you," I said.

As Jerry and the other driver moved our cars out of the way

the passenger showed the security guy ID that I didn't get a look at. It must have been good because the guard backed right off.

We walked over to where Jerry and the other driver were waiting.

Both the strangers were in their thirties, wearing off-the-rack suits and skinny ties. They didn't look like Secret Service to me, or FBI.

"Mind if we see those IDs?" I asked.

The men exchanged a glance, then took out their folders, flashed us Palm Springs police department buzzers. The passenger was Dugan, and the driver was Atkins.

"What the hell—" I said.

"Detective Stanze would like to see you fellas now that you're back in town," Dugan said.

Atkins looked at Jerry. "Bet you're gonna have to explain about that gun."

"Bet you're gonna have ta explain about your black eye," Jerry said.

"I don't have a—" Atkins said, then suddenly backed away from Jerry warily. "I could take you in for manhandling me."

"You're right," I said, "he jerked you out of the car pretty easily. Want to explain that? That'd leave a bruised ego."

"Look," Dugan said, "we were just sort of escortin' you back. You know, keepin' an eye on you like Stanze asked."

"So you didn't follow us from L.A.?" I asked, just to confirm.

"No, we picked you up when you got to Palm Springs," Dugan said.

"You friends with Frank Sinatra?" Atkins asked.

"Yeah, we are."

"Umm," Dugan said, "that blonde in your car, was that . . . Marilyn Monroe?"

"No," I said, "it was Mamie Van Doren. Why don't you call Stanze and tell him we'll be in a little later. We're gonna freshen up first."

"Yeah, you guys can go back home to paradise," Jerry said.

"It is paradise," Atkins said. "Where are you from, bub?"

"New York, pal," Jerry said, "and you can keep yer sand and sun. I'll take the Great White Way, thanks."

Atkins made a move as if he was going to poke Jerry in the chest with his finger, but he drew it back at the last minute. Wise decision. Jerry probably would have pulled it off and shoved it up the guy's ass.

"Let's go," Dugan said to his partner. "We're done here. We were doin' a favor for your guy, Stanze."

"He's not my guy."

"Well, whatever he is, tell him not to call us again. We're done cooperatin'." He turned to Jerry. "You ever point a gun at me again—"

Jerry stopped him by drawing the gun and pointing it at him.

Atkins looked at Dugan, then they both chuckled, shook their heads and walked away.

Thirty-two

WHEN WE GOT BACK to Marilyn's house I used the key she gave us to get into the guesthouse. We walked through and out the back door to a small patio.

"Jerry, you're gonna have to cool it with the gun unless we really need it."

"I didn't know they was cops, Mr. G."

"I know, but how about the second time?"

"The guy just pissed me off."

"Okay, well, I've got to go and see Detective Stanze and try to explain all this. Meanwhile, I'll have him explain why he's havin' me followed."

"I better come with ya, Mr. G.," Jerry said. "You're gonna hafta explain me, too."

"Let me see if I can deal with it," I suggested. "I know how allergic to cops you are. If I can't, then you'll have to go in and talk to him. I'll try to keep you out of it, but . . ."

"I get it. Thanks, Mr. G."

"Sure. Just stay here, have somethin' to eat, watch TV. I'll be back as soon as I can."

"You got it, Mr. G."

* * *

A uniformed cop walked me to Stanze's desk.

"Mr. Gianelli," he said. "Nice of you to drop by."

"I assume you heard from your Palm Springs buddies?" I asked. "Dugan and . . . what was it, Atkins?"

Another cop came walking over, plainclothes, white hair, deep tan.

"Say hello to my partner, Detective Bailey."

"Dave Bailey," the man said. "Hey."

"Let's go someplace and talk," Stanze suggested.

"Need me?" Bailey asked.

"Nah, I got it," Stanze said. "The lieutenant in?"

"No."

"I'm gonna use his office."

"He's gonna catch you one of these days," Bailey said.

"I'm just tryin' his chair on for size," Stanze said. To me, "Come on."

When we got into the office, he closed the door, walked around and sat in his boss's chair again. I sat across from him.

"You got ambitions," I said.

"Who doesn't?"

"Would you like to tell me why you were havin' me followed?"

"Followed?" Stanze asked. "Those officers were there for your protection."

"Protection from what?"

"Or who?" he asked. "How about whoever made your friend go missing?"

"I didn't ask for protection."

"No, that's right, you have your own. Who's the guy with the gun, Gianelli?"

"What happened to the 'mister'?" I asked.

"Maybe you can earn it back, *comprende*?" the detective

said. I was willing to bet that was the only Spanish he knew. "Who's your friend?"

"He came to watch my back."

"He got a permit for that gun?"

"I'm sure he does."

"Where's he from?"

"New York."

"How'd he get a gun here from New York?"

"In his luggage, I assume."

"Why didn't you bring him in with you?"

"Did you want to see him?" I asked. "I thought this was between you and me."

"What did the Palm Springs detectives tell you?"

"Oh, yeah, they gave me a message for you," I said. "They said don't call them again. So tell me, how did they know we were in Palm Springs? Were you havin' me followed here and your guys lost me?"

"Come on," he said, standing up.

"Where?"

"Downstairs to see your friend."

"My friend?"

"Yeah," Stanze said. "He was picked up ten minutes after you left him at Marilyn Monroe's house."

I got to my feet fast. "What the hell for?"

"He pointed a gun at a cop," Stanze said. "Two cops, as a matter of fact."

"We didn't know they were cops," I said. "They could've been the guys who made my friend disappear. Isn't that what you said? Somebody made him disappear?"

"I'm looking into it," Stanze said. "What were you doing in Palm Springs?"

"What do you think?"

"I think you took Marilyn Monroe somewhere. Why?"

"She's a friend of mine," I said. "I didn't want any of this spilling over on to her."

"Look, I assume you were candid with me in our first meeting," Stanze said. "So you took Miss Monroe someplace safe? What did you do? Put her in a motel?"

"Marilyn Monroe in a motel?" I asked.

"Okay, come on," Stanze said. "Let's go downstairs and see your guy."

"You're not gonna arrest him, are you?"

"Let's see if he's got that permit."

Thirty-three

WE WENT DOWN TO a holding cell where they had Jerry, who was sitting on a bunk, looking very calm. Outside the cell was the uniformed turnkey and another uniformed cop.

"Open it," Stanze told the turnkey.

"Yes, sir."

He opened the cell door, then backed away. Stanze entered and I followed.

"Mr. Epstein," Stanze said, "my name is Detective Stanze."

Jerry looked up at him.

"Mr. Gianelli has explained to me that you didn't know the two men were cops when you pointed your gun at them. Is that correct?"

I had no idea what I'd done but apparently I'd earned back my "mister."

"He's right."

"I need to see your pistol permit."

"It's with my stuff," Jerry said, "which they took away from me."

Detective Stanze turned to the cop standing outside the cell.

"Get me his things."

"Yes, sir."

He looked at Jerry. "Is there any point in me asking you the same questions I asked Mr. Gianelli?"

"Whatever Mr. G. said, I agree with."

"That's what I thought. What do you do in Brooklyn, Mr. Epstein?"

"This and that."

Stanze looked at me. "Why is it every time I ask one of these guys what they do they say 'this and that,'" he asked me.

"What guys are those?"

"One of these torpedoes," Stanze said, "or hard guys, or whatever they call themselves these days. Gunsel. Wiseguys. Isn't that what they call them back east?"

"I ain't a wiseguy," Jerry said, "and I'm nobody's torpedo."

"Oh, sensitive, huh?"

The cops returned with an envelope holding Jerry's things. There was a table in the cell, so Stanze emptied the envelope onto it. Wallet, some change, a key ring with three keys. No gun. Jerry had not been dumb enough to carry it into the police station.

Stanze picked up the wallet. He went through it, found the permit and studied it.

"You know this is no good in the state of California," he said.

"I know."

"And yet you were carrying a gun."

"I was gonna come in and register it," Jerry said, "but I got busy."

"Uh-huh. With Marilyn Monroe?"

"I'm just helpin' Miss M."

"Do what?"

"Stay safe."

"Why did you point your gun at those two Palm Springs cops—*after* they identified themselves?"

"They was bein' assholes."

"They could have taken you in, you know."

"They was out of their jurisdiction."

"Oh, you know the law?"

"Some."

"Well, I'm not out of my jurisdiction."

"I ain't carrin' it now."

"But you were, earlier today. You admitted it."

"I'd be stupid to deny it," Jerry said, "with them two Palm Springs dicks tellin' you I pointed it at them."

"For being assholes."

"Yup."

Stanze looked at me.

"They were," I said. "I was there."

Stanze put the wallet back on the table. He didn't put the items back into the envelope. I took that as a good sign.

"What have you done about finding Danny Bardini?" I asked. "Have you been back to that motel?"

"I talked to the owner," he answered. "He says he checked the records. There's no sign of anyone by that name signing in."

"Somebody could've erased it," I said. "Did you check the airport?"

"Yes, your friend did fly into L.A. on the same flight with Miss Monroe. That's the reason I believe you, that and I'm sure that clerk I talked to was lying through his teeth."

"Is he still around?"

"He is. I saw him there earlier, when I talked to the owner."

"He'd be silly to run," Jerry said. "That'd prove he was a liar."

"Very good, gunsel," Stanze said.

Jerry took the name-calling impassively. The only one he really didn't like was "torpedo."

"Okay," Stanze said, "pick up your stuff and go."

Jerry collected his belongings and pocketed them.

"You never answered my question," I said.

"What question was that?"

"Were you havin' us followed until we left L.A.? And did your guys lose us?"

"If I was having you followed it was for your own protection."

"That's what the Palm Springs dicks said," Jerry said.

"You fellas going to be at Miss Monroe's house, even though she's not there? I mean, if I want to reach you again?"

"Yeah, we'll be there," I said. "She gave me a key. We got permission."

"Okay, then," he said. "If I find out anything about your friend, I'll call you there."

"Thanks."

He walked us out of the cell block and upstairs to the main floor. Before I could leave he grabbed my arm.

"You did drop Miss Monroe off at Frank Sinatra's, right?"

"Why would I have done that, Detective?" I asked. "Didn't you hear? They broke up."

Thirty-four

WHEN WE WALKED INTO the office of the motel the skinny girl behind the desk looked at Jerry with wide eyes. He was big, and was wearing a sports jacket. Even though I was used to the heat—being from Vegas—I had taken my jacket off and left it in the car.

"Who owns this joint?" Jerry demanded loudly.

"Um, um, Mr. Cohen," the frightened girl replied.

"Where is he?"

"Um, he's in—in the back." She jerked her finger toward a doorway.

"Thanks."

He stormed past the girl toward the doorway.

"Uh, you can't—" she started, but I stopped her.

"Don't bother," I said. "You'll just make him mad."

I followed Jerry through the door, found him facing a guy in a tank top seated in a leather lounge chair. The guy was in his sixties, with buzz-cut white hair and white stubble. He had good biceps on him for his age, but his gut hung over a cheap belt.

"What the hell—" he started.

He tried to get up but Jerry put a massive hand on the guy's chest and shoved him back down. He kept his hand on the man's chest. The guy grabbed Jerry's wrist with both hands and strained, but despite the good biceps he couldn't budge it.

"Whataya want?" he demanded.

"Just answer a few questions," I said to him, "and we'll go away."

The guy looked at me.

"You his keeper?" he demanded. "Tell him to stop crushing my chest."

"I ain't his keeper," I said, "but I might be able to persuade him, if you're willing to talk to us."

"I ain't gonna be talkin' to nobody if he crushes my damn chest!" He looked up at Jerry. "It's a crime I should breathe?"

"Okay, Jerry," I said. "Let him breathe."

Jerry removed his hand.

"Jesus!"

"Are you Cohen?"

"Yeah, Stanley Cohen. Who're you? I don't owe no book-ies."

"We're not collectin' on the debt, Mr. Cohen," I said.

"Well, you ain't cops."

"No, not cops."

"Then what?"

"I told you. Somebody with questions."

"I ain't answerin' no questions—oof—" He got cut off when Jerry clamped his hand back on Cohen's chest. "Jesus, awright already."

Jerry removed his hand.

"Whataya wanna know?"

"The cops were here talking to you about one of your desk clerks."

"Yeah. So?"

"We want his name and address."

"Why?"

"Because he's lyin' to the cops, and to you, and we want the truth."

"Max don't lie to me."

"Okay, then you're lyin', too," I said. "Jerry, the man's lyin'. Make him tell the truth."

Jerry reached down for the guy, this time with both hands. Cohen squawked, put his hands up in front of his face and said, "Awright, awright, call 'im off!"

"Jerry."

The big guy backed off.

"Johnson, Max Johnson," Cohen said. "That's his name."

"We need his address."

"Can I get up?"

"Sure," I said.

Cohen eyed Jerry warily as he got to his feet. He walked to a cabinet, opened it and removed an index card. Turning, he held it out to me.

"Here, take it. I'm gonna fire his ass anyway."

"Why?" I asked.

"Because he brought you guys here," Cohen said. "He brought the cops here. This I don't need."

"So what about Danny Bardini?" I asked. "Was he registered here or not?"

Cohen put his hands out, as if to ward us off, and said, "I really don't know about that. Max said he never registered, and I believed him. When the cops showed up askin' questions I didn't know what the hell was goin' on, and now that you guys are here I still don't. What's the big deal if the guy stayed here or not?"

"He's missing," I said. "That's what the big deal is."

"Well, I don't see no record that he was ever here. I'm sorry."

"Max Johnson told me he was here for four days."

"Well then, Max musta got rid of the registration card."

"Let's go," I said to Jerry. I looked at Cohen. "If you call

Johnson and warn him we're comin' we'll be back—and I won't hold my friend here back."

"I got it," Cohen said. "Believe me, I got it."

"And don't let your girl out there make any calls, either."

"She don't know nothin'," Cohen said.

"Oh, one more thing," I said. "We need to talk to two of your other clerks. Hilary? Is that the girl outside? And Harry."

"I got no Hilary and no Harry," Cohen said. "I guess Max really was a liar."

I looked at Jerry and we turned and left.

"Well, we didn't get anything to prove to Stanze that Danny was here."

"It sounded to me like he believed ya already," Jerry said, leaning against the car.

"Maybe," I said, "but let's find this Johnson guy and confirm it."

"You got it, Mr. G."

Thirty-five

WHEN WE GOT IN the car Jerry asked, "What's the address?"
I read it off for him.

"How do we get there?"

"I don't know," I said.

"We could ask directions."

"We're from Brooklyn," I said, "we don't ask directions."

"Well, then . . . how are we gonna get there?"

I looked at him. "We'll ask for directions."

After we stopped at a gas station for help we drove to an apartment building on the outskirts of Brentwood.

"I thought Brentwood was all rich people and movie stars," Jerry said, parking in front of the building.

"So did I."

"So where did this block come from?"

"This must be the Brentwood slums."

"I'm glad I have my gun," he said.

"You do?" I asked. "But . . . in the police station . . ."

"I left it in the trunk."

"The trunk?" I said. "Of my car?"

"Well, I didn't think they'd search your car," he said. "Why would they?"

"Yeah," I said, "why would they?"

Trying a second look at the building, I decided it probably was a good thing that Jerry had his gun.

We opened the trunk and he dug the .45 out of the wheel well, stuck it in his belt.

"No holster?"

"That would've looked suspicious," he said. "I mean, if I was wearing an empty holster?"

We started toward the building, and I put my hand on his arm to stop him.

"When exactly did you put the gun in the trunk?"

"Before you drove to the police station."

"Why?"

"I had a bad feelin'."

"A bad feelin'?"

"Yeah, that they was gonna pick me up. I figured those assholes from Palm Springs was gonna squeal."

We walked to the building. There were doorbells, but only a few had names on them.

"Jerry."

"Yeah, Mr. G.?"

"The next time you have a bad feelin' will you let me know?"

"Sure, Mr. G."

We tried the front door and it was unlocked. In fact, the lock was broken.

"Mr. G.?"

"Yeah."

"This is it," he said. "I got a bad feelin' about this."

"Mmm, me, too."

We went in. The urine smell was enough to make my eyes sting.

"What apartment?" he asked.

I looked at the index card.

"Two-C."

"Second floor."

We went up the steps, walked past only one apartment that seemed to be occupied. A radio was playing, and a child was wailing. When we got to 2C Jerry drew his gun.

"Me first, Mr. G."

I nodded.

He reached for the doorknob and it turned easily.

"This has got to be a phony address," I said.

"Why?" Jerry asked. "When the guy got the job at the motel why would he give a phony address?"

"I don't know," I said. "Maybe . . ."

He pushed the door open and went in quickly with the gun held out in front of him. I waited until he waved me in.

I left the door open and looked around. There was a sagging sofa with one broken leg and an armchair with half the stuffing sticking out. Off to the left was a folding table with a slightly limp fourth leg.

"Nobody even bothered to try and make it look lived in," Jerry said.

"There's a kitchen, and another room. Bedroom?"

"We better check," he said.

I nodded.

"You take the kitchen, Mr. G."

"Right."

No body, I thought, thank God there was no body.

I entered the kitchen. Cabinet doors were hanging off their hinges or missing completely; there was a kitchen table but no chairs. The stove was minus two burners. I opened the oven and looked in, found it empty and dirty.

No bodies. I went back into the living room.

"Jerry?"

"Yeah?"

"Anything?"

He came out of the bedroom, tucking the .45 into his belt.

"Nothing, Mr. G. There's a chest of drawers, but nothing's been in them for a long time."

"So it's a phony address."

"Oh, yeah."

"That doesn't make any sense," I said. "Who gets a job at a fleabag motel and gives a phony address?"

"When was he hired?" Jerry asked.

"Oh, yeah," I said, remembering the index card. "He was hired . . . a week ago."

"Before Danny got to L.A."

"Yeah."

"Odd," he said.

"I think so."

"Can we get out of here now, Mr. G.?" he asked. "My eyes are burnin' something bad."

"Yeah, let's go," I said, "before a body falls from the ceiling."

We stopped at a Chinese takeout and brought two greasy bags of food and a six-pack back to Marilyn's guesthouse.

"Before we go inside," I said, "we've got something to decide."

"Like what?"

"Whether or not we believe the house is bugged," I said. "And if the house is bugged, is the guesthouse bugged?"

"What do you say?" he asked.

"I think if they bugged the main house there's no point in bugging the guesthouse."

"I agree."

"You do?"

"Well, no . . . but I want to eat this Chinks hot. I gotta think if one house is bugged, so's the other one, Mr. G."

"Good point," I said. "We'll just have to watch our p's and q's then."

"Sure, Mr. G."

Thirty-six

CHINKS?" I ASKED INSIDE. "When did you start callin' it that?"

Jerry shrugged. "Did it since I was a kid. I probably heard somebody else do it. Why?"

"My grandmother use to call it that," I said.

We opened all the containers, got some plates and sat down at the table to demolish the food along with bottles of Schlitz. And just in case the house was bugged, we kept the water running in the sink for background noise.

"I was hoping we'd find out something from the desk clerk," I said.

"Maybe we should go back," Jerry said. "Maybe the owner was lying."

"I don't think so," I said, "not with your hand on his chest."

"Well, he's gotta have a good phone number to reach the guy at," Jerry said. "It's gotta be on that card. Maybe we should call it and see?"

"Good idea."

I swallowed the egg roll I was chewing, went to the phone

and fished that index card out of my pocket. I dialed the number. After twenty rings I hung up.

"No answer," I said, sitting back down. "We're lookin' at a brick wall, Jerry."

I watched Jerry pick up a wonton with his chopsticks. I was using a fork.

"I could never get the hang of that," I said, indicating his sticks.

"I eat lots of Chinks," he said.

"So do I. My grandmother—the only member of my family who wasn't crazy—tried to show me how to use them when I was a kid. She lived in Little Italy and took me to Chinatown a lot."

"Ya want I should show ya?"

"No, that's okay," I said. "I do pretty well with a fork."

I emptied pepper steak onto my plate and took a swig of beer.

"If this was Vegas I might have some idea about what to do, where to look," I said, "but I'm out of my element here."

"What about what you said before?" Jerry asked, dumping a bunch of fried rice onto his plate.

"About what?"

"Hirin' a PI." He lowered his voice. "That Otash guy?"

"Yeah, I was thinkin' about that."

"We could go see him tomorrow . . . unless ya wanna ask that detective to recommend somebody."

"I don't think we want Stanze knowin' that we're hirin' a PI," I said. "He doesn't want us messin' in his business."

"But it ain't his business, Mr. G.," Jerry said. "It's your business. But I know what ya mean. Cops always think stuff's their business when it ain't."

"Okay," I said, "so we'll go talk to Otash tomorrow. I'll call Dean first."

"Whataya wanna call him for?"

"I'm involved because he asked me to be, and Danny's missin' because I asked him to help. I'll ask Dean to call Otash and arrange an appointment. That way we'll know that he'll see us."

"That sounds like a good idea, Mr. G." He grabbed the fried rice box, then looked at me. "You like the steamed white or the fried?"

"I'll take the white."

"Good," he said, "I like the fried." He emptied the box onto his plate, then dumped chicken chow mein on top of it.

"I'll call Dean after we finish eating," I said. "You want this last egg roll?"

"Sure," he said, taking it.

Why did I ask?

"Hey, Eddie," Dean said when Jeannie put him on the phone. I was surprised he was home. I thought Jeannie would have to give me a phone number wherever he was performing. "Lucky you caught me home. I'm heading for Chicago tomorrow to do a show. Is this about Marilyn?"

"It started with Marilyn, Dean," I said. "Now it's moved on."

I'd had to drive three blocks before I found a pay phone, but I didn't want to call from the house.

I told him what had been going on and asked him about Otash.

"I know Fred, of course," he said, "but you should know that he's a hustler. That's why you see so many of his ads in the paper."

"A hustler?" I asked. "You mean . . . he's on the hustle?"

"No, he's a con man. He'll work for anybody who pays him. If he was a lawyer you'd call him an ambulance chaser."

"But is he any good?"

"As far as I know," Dean said, "he's very good. If you need someone who knows his way around California, he's your man."

"I need someone who knows somethin' about findin' a missing person."

"Then use him," Dean said. "You want me to call him?"

"Yeah," I said, "can you do it first thing in the mornin'?"

"Sure thing. You bringing Big Jerry with you?"

"Yeah, he's here."

"Okay," Dean said, "I'll tell Fred to expect both of you. I'll tell him it would be a favor to me."

"Don't ask him to do it for free," I said.

"I wouldn't think of it," he said. "Fred Otash doesn't work for anybody for free."

"Okay, thanks. Hey, Dean?"

"Yeah, pally?"

"What did you mean when you said he'd work for anybody?" I asked.

"I meant," Dean said, "that he will work for *anybody*."

"Uh-huh," I said. "Okay, thanks."

"No, thank *you*, Eddie," Dean said. "I know I got you into this, which means I got Danny into this. I hope you find him okay."

I hung up just as my time ran out.

Thirty-seven

FRED OTASH'S OFFICE WAS in Hollywood, on North Laurel Avenue. We took the elevator up and presented ourselves to a woman who looked as if she was dressed for an audition rather than a day at work. Her nails and lips were bloodred, her hair Jayne Mansfield blond, her dress a size too small and protesting.

"Yes?"

"We'd like to see Mr. Otash."

"Do you have an appointment?"

"Yes."

"Your name?"

"Gianelli, Eddie Gianelli?"

She opened her appointment book, looked at it and shook her head. "I don't have you in my book, sir."

"Why don't you call Fred and ask him?" I suggested. "He got a call this morning from Dean Martin to set this up."

She let loose with a heavy sigh that tested the resolve of her dress, got a put-upon look on her face and pressed the intercom button.

"Mr. Otash, there's a Mr. Gianelli here who says Dean Martin called—"

"Send him in, Leona," a voice said, "and his friend, too."

She hung up and tapped her appointment book with her red nails. Clearly, this was not acceptable behavior to her. "You can go in."

"Thank you."

There was only one other door so we opened it and stepped through. Fred Otash stood up, remained behind his desk, and extended his hand. He wasn't short, had wavy dark hair and a full face. He looked more like an agent than a private eye.

"Mr. Gianelli?"

"That's right." I shook his hand.

"And Mr. Epstein?"

"Hiya," Jerry said, shaking his hand.

"Wow, you're a big one," Otash said. "Have a seat."

We both sat. The chairs were cushioned and comfortable. The office was expensively furnished in dark wood that gleamed. I wondered if the red-nailed secretary also did the dusting.

"Well, okay," he said, "Dean tells me you're friends of his who need help. He also told me you're in trouble because you were helping him. It all sounds real involved, so whenever you're ready . . . go!"

I started with Dean asking me to help Marilyn and worked my way through everything. The only thing I left out was why I went to New York.

When I was done he asked, "Why did you go to New York?"

"Is that relevant?"

"I don't know," he said, "and I won't know until you tell me."

"A funeral," I said. "Family."

"Whose?"

I looked at him.

"Okay, never mind that part," he said, waving a hand. "You say Danny Bardini is in my business?"

"That's right."

"I don't know him," he said with a frown. This seemed to bother him. "Okay, never mind. What we have to do here is move on."

"You'll take the case?" Jerry asked.

Otash nodded. "As long as there's no major open police case that I'd be interfering in."

"Not that I know of."

"I'll have my girl type up a standard contract for you. After we take care of the business aspect of this, I'm all yours."

Thirty-eight

I SIGNED OTASH'S CONTRACT and agreed to his fee. I had no idea if he was giving us any kind of discount or not because of Dean, but he seemed expensive.

"All right, gentlemen," he said, when Leona left with the signed document and I had a copy in my pocket. "Do you have any objection to my talking to Detective Stanze?"

"Do you know him?" I asked.

"No," he said, "but I do know a few guys at the West Los Angeles Station."

"Anyone with rank?" I asked.

"Yes."

"I don't want to thumb my nose at this detective," I said.

"Leave it to me," he said. "I can talk to him without damaging his ego. And believe me, he'd probably rather I do this than you flounder around on your own. No offense."

"None taken," Jerry said.

Otash looked at him. "That's good, big guy," he said. "I'd hate to offend you." He looked at me, pushed a pad of lined paper my way. "I need the address of that motel, the name of the manager, the clerk, the address you had on the clerk . . . any place else you've already gone."

"Okay."

"Any objection to my talking with Miss Monroe?"

"No," I said, "but I'll have to set that up. She's . . . delicate."

"So I hear," Otash said. "I've dealt with stars before, Mr. Gianelli. I know how to handle them."

"That may be," I said, "but I'll still have to set it up. If you want to talk to her in person, I'll have to be there."

"That's fine with me. Where is she now?"

Oh, yeah, I had left out that part. I hesitated.

"Is that something you don't want to tell me?" he asked.

"Um, no," I said. "She's in Palm Springs, staying with . . . a friend."

"Uh-huh," he said. "Okay, well I'll start with the police, and then look into that motel. Oh, and would you write down there a complete description of your friend?"

"Sure." I wrote down as complete a description as I could.

"Very good," Otash said, accepting the pad back.

"If you gentlemen don't mind I'd like to ask what Mr. Epstein's interest in all this is?"

"He's with me," I said.

"Yes, but why?"

"I help Mr. G. when he needs help," Jerry said.

"You don't sound like you're from Vegas," Otash said.

"I'm from New York."

"Brooklyn, if my ear is right."

"That's right."

Otash looked at me. "Did you know each other when you lived in Brooklyn?"

"No," I said, "we only met a couple of years ago, in Vegas."

"I see."

"My relationship with Jerry has no bearing on what we're doin' here, Mr. Otash," I said. "He just volunteered to come here and help me."

Otash nodded. "Very well then," he said. "Where can I contact you?"

"We're staying in Marilyn Monroe's guesthouse," I said. "I've written the number down there."

"Excellent," Otash said. "I'll try to have something for you by the end of the day."

"Thank you," I said, standing up. Jerry did the same. We both shook hands with Otash again, and then he walked us to his door.

"Will you fellas be staying in, or . . . going sightseeing? Something?"

"We're not interested in sightseeing," I said, "but we might be in and out."

"I see. Well, if I don't get you the first time I'll just try again."

"That'd be good."

We walked past the secretary, who didn't pay any attention to us, and left.

"What'd you think?" I asked, when we got to the street.

"I don't like him," Jerry said. "He's too slick."

"Like an agent," I said.

"Or a lawyer," Jerry said. "He asks a lot of questions."

"Part of his job."

"Yeah, but why does it matter why I'm here?"

"I don't know," I said. "He does seem to need a lot of information. Maybe he's just bein' thorough."

"Yeah," Jerry said, "maybe. So what do we do now?"

"You got any suggestions?"

"I do," he said, "but you probably won't like it."

Since we'd only had toast and coffee for breakfast I thought I knew.

"Let's go find some pancakes," I said.

A big grin split Jerry face.

"There ya go, Mr. G."

Thirty-nine

WE STOPPED AT A pay phone before we went back to the guesthouse so I could call Penny, who proceeded to read me the riot act for taking so long to get back to her. I didn't bother mentioning that Jerry and I had stopped for pancakes. That really would have set her off.

I told her what we had been doing and who we'd hired to help us.

"Fred Otash?" she asked. "Danny hates him."

"He knows him?"

"No, he *knows* of him and doesn't like him one bit," she said.

"Jealous?"

She made a noise into the phone. "You know Danny. That's not it. The guy has a reputation and it ain't all good. Why don't you let me give you some names?"

"I think I'll stick with Otash for now, Penny."

"By the way," she asked, "how is Miss Monroe?"

"She's in Palm Springs, and I'm in L.A."

"Where are you staying?"

"In her guesthouse."

"Let me have the number so I can get in touch with you."

"Are you still not goin' back to the office?" I asked.

"I don't think so," she said. "It's . . . too depressing. I'll just close the office and wait for you to call me."

"Okay, Penny. As soon as I know something."

"And say hi to Jerry for me. I'm glad he's there with you."

"So am I."

I hung up and looked at Jerry. "She says hi."

"Cute kid," he said.

"Yeah."

"So," he said, "now that we got this guy Otash workin' on it, what do we do? Go back to Vegas?"

"No," I said, "I'm thinkin' we go out to Palm Springs to see Marilyn."

"Bring her back here?"

"I don't think so," I said. "I mean, we haven't done a thing about finding out who's watchin' her. We've been spendin' all our time tryin' to find Danny."

"Same thing, ain't it?" he asked. "Find out who's watchin' her we find out who disappeared Danny."

"Yeah, maybe."

"You don't think so?"

"Danny's worked on a lot of cases, Jerry," I said. "What if somebody from one of those spotted him here in L.A. and way-laid him."

"That'd be a helluva coincidence, Mr. G.," Jerry said. "I think we're better off figurin' it's all connected. But hey, you're the brains, I'm just the muscle."

"Yeah," I said, "I'm the brains, that's why I didn't think of calling Penny at home sooner."

"Hey, I didn't think of it either, Mr. G."

"Yeah, but you're just muscle," I said. "You said it yourself."

"I was jus' tryin' ta make you feel better, Mr. G.," he said, straight-faced.

"Speaking of calling, I better call Marilyn and make sure she's okay," I said. "Maybe we won't need to drive out there."

Luckily, I had started carrying a lot of change.

"Sinatra residence," George said.

"Hey, George, it's Eddie G. How's it goin' there?" I asked.

"We've had some excitement here, sir."

"What kind of excitement, George?"

"I better let Mr. Sinatra tell you himself."

I heard him put the phone down, and moments later Frank picked it up.

"Hey, Eddie."

"What's goin' on, Frank?"

"We had somebody on the grounds last night," Frank said. "A couple of my guys saw him near the house and chased him."

"Catch him?"

"No, he got away."

"How's Marilyn?"

"She was a little shook up, but I convinced her that it had more to do with JFK's visit than with her," he said.

"Did she buy it?"

"I think so."

"Do you buy it?"

"Not sure about that, buddy boy," he said.

"Okay, I think Jerry and I will take a ride out there so I can talk to her."

"That's a good idea," he said. "She depends on you a lot, Eddie. And when Marilyn starts depending on you, you've really got your hands full. Believe me, I know."

"Okay, Frank. We should be there in a couple of hours."

"Plan on eatin' and spendin' the night, pal," Frank said. "No arguments."

"Sure, Frank," I said. "No arguments."

Forty

WHEN WE GOT TO PALM SPRINGS Marilyn hugged both of us—but I told myself she hugged me longer and harder.

We had cannelloni with her and Frank and then, while Frank took Jerry to see his Oscar, I sat outside by the pool with Marilyn. We weren't dressed to go swimming. She was wearing jeans with the legs rolled up her shins and a short-sleeved top. I had on a sports shirt and some chinos. We sat facing each other on two lounge chairs.

"Heard you had some excitement last night," I said.

"Is that why you came back?" she asked. "To see if I was a mess?"

"I came back to see if you were all right, Marilyn."

"So you don't have any news?"

"No, not really," I said, "but we've got somebody workin' on it with us. A professional."

"Who?"

I didn't want to tell her his name. She might have heard of Otash, which meant she might have heard some unflattering things.

"Don't worry about it," I said. "It's somebody who's gonna work hard for us."

"What about your friend, Danny? Any sign of him, yet?" she asked.

"No, not yet."

She put her hand on my knee. "I'm sorry, Eddie."

I put my hand over hers. "He'll turn up," I said. "I'm sure of it."

"Well, Frank thinks that the prowler last night had something to do with Jack's visit."

"He's probably right, since that's no secret to anyone."

"Has anyone been around my house?"

"Not that we've seen," I said.

"Are you staying in the main house?"

"No, out back."

"Both of you?" her eyes went wide. "Why, that little house is barely big enough for Jerry. Eddie, you stay in my house." Then she got excited, as if she'd just thought of something. She literally bounced up and down. "Sleep in my bed, Eddie!"

God, a week ago if someone had told me I'd hear those words from Marilyn Monroe . . .

"That's okay, Marilyn—"

"Well, sleep on the sofa, then, it's nice and big. I often curl up on it to watch TV and end up there all night."

"I can do that," I said. I didn't want to tell her we thought her house was bugged, and that's why we weren't using it.

"How are you doin' with Frank?"

"He's being very sweet, but he's real busy with the construction. I can't believe all the work he's doing. I hope the president appreciates it."

"I hope so, too."

"Eddie"—she moved her hand up and down my leg—"I know you're doing a lot for me already, but could I ask you a favor?"

"Of course you can." I put my hand on hers to stop hers from moving. I didn't think she really knew what she was doing.

"It's about Clark, and people saying I . . . I killed him."

"I thought we talked about that, Marilyn."

"I know, I know we did, but . . . could you go and talk to Kay for me?"

"What do you want me to say?"

"I want you to find out if she blames me . . . for anything. I don't care about the newspaper gossips, but I'd hate it if Kay thought badly of me. She and I got along so well on the set. We called Clark 'our man.' It would just kill me if she thought I'd ever hurt him."

"Marilyn, why press it—"

She grabbed my hand and squeezed.

"Please, Eddie. I—I need this. I can't sleep. I need to know she doesn't blame me."

She brought her other hand into play, grabbing mine in both of hers and moving it onto her leg, where she held it tightly.

"All right," I said, helpless because of the pleading look in her eyes, "all right, I'll go and talk to her."

"Oh, Eddie, thank you."

She threw herself at me, hugging me tightly, knocking me back onto the lounger with her on top of me. Little sister or not, I was very much aware that I had Marilyn Monroe's braless breasts pressing tightly against me.

"Hey, what goes on out here?" Frank called out.

Marilyn was giggling as she got into a seated position. She adjusted herself and stood up.

"Eddie just made me a very happy woman," she announced.

Frank looked at me and said, "That didn't take very long."

"Screw you, Frank," I said. It felt good to laugh.

Forty-one

JERRY HAD A BEER in one hand and what looked like bourbon in the other, while Frank held up highballs, one of which had a cherry in it.

"Me and Jerry decided we had to drink to good friends," Frank said, handing Marilyn the drink with the cherry.

"Here ya go, Mr. G.," Jerry said, handing me the bourbon.

"Thanks, Jerry," I said, standing up and accepting the glass.

"There's nothin' like good friends," Frank announced, holding his glass up.

"Here, here," I said.

After toasting each other we sat and talked for a while. An hour or so later Marilyn decided to turn in. She kissed us each good night, but the kiss on Frank's cheek could only be described as a peck. She kissed Jerry on the cheek, and hugged him around the neck, not letting him get up. Then she came to me and pressed her silky cheek to mine, then kissed me at the corner of my mouth. After a moment she looked me right in the eyes and said breathily, "Good night, Eddie."

"Night, kid."

She went off to bed and we had another drink. Then Jerry announced he was going to turn in.

"Want George to show you the way, Jerry?" Frank asked.

"No, thanks, Mr. S., I can find it. I just gotta walk past the plaque that says 'President Kennedy Slept Here.' Night Mr. G."

"Night, Jerry."

"Guess I'll have to move that plaque when Jack sleeps in the new wing," Frank said. "Want another drink, Eddie?"

"I think I'm done, Frank."

"Aw, c'mon, one more. I wanna talk to you about a couple of things."

"Okay, one more."

"I'll get 'em," Frank said, getting up from his lounge chair and quickly going inside. He was back in a few moments with two drinks.

"What do you need, Frank?" I asked.

"This thing with Marilyn," he said. "I think she might be fallin' for you."

"Aw, come on, Frank. I'm not a ballplayer, or a playwright, or . . . or you."

"She don't care about that," he said. "Right now you're the man in her life, the one she's clinging to. I played that role for a while, but I couldn't cut it. Joe D., he still tries even though they're divorced. But it's you, right now. Be careful."

"Frank, I'm not gonna get involved with her. I mean, I'm not gonna sleep with her."

He laughed. "How you gonna resist if she throws herself at you?"

"She's too fragile, Frank," I said. "I don't want to hurt her, and I don't know if I could handle her full time, you know?"

"Believe me, I know. Look, I'm just givin' you a friendly warning. What you do is your business."

"I appreciate it, Frank."

Frank remained standing, looking out over the pool. I didn't know if he was staring at the construction work, or . . . just staring.

"Hey, Frank, what happened with that book you were readin' last year? You were thinkin' of makin' it into a movie?" I tried lightening the mood.

"Which one?"

"The detective one."

"Oh, *Miami Mayhem*, the one about the private eye, Tony Rome."

"Yeah, that's it."

"Well I'd like to make it, but it's gonna have to wait. I got a lot of films comin' up, and I'm readin' this other book called *Von Ryan's Express* that I'd really like to do, but . . ."

"But what?"

He looked at me.

"I've been makin' movies left and right since *From Here to Eternity*. Most of them made money, some of them were even good. Guess I was thinkin' make 'em while I can, you know? Ya never know when it could all be taken away from you . . . again."

I was uncomfortable. I'd never seen Frank anything but confident.

"Lately I'm thinkin' I should just stick to what I do best, you know? I'm a saloon singer. Maybe I should leave the movies to other guys."

"You can't do that, Frank."

"Why not?"

"People love your films," I said. "Jesus, *Some Came Running, Pal Joey, Johnny Concho*—"

"*Concho*," Frank said. "Wow, there was a stinker."

"I like that movie!" I said indignantly.

"Really?"

"What about *Guys and Dolls*?"

"That was Brando's movie."

"*High Society?*"

"Fluff," he said, "somebody wanted me and Crosby in a movie together, but who was lookin' at us when Grace Kelly was on the screen?"

"Okay then, *The Man with the Golden Arm.* You were great in that!"

"Yeah, okay, that was a good one."

"See? You gotta keep makin' movies, Frank."

"Well, a lot is gonna depend on the one I just finished."

"What's that?"

"It's called *The Manchurian Candidate.* It's a little different than anything else I've done. It's got a message."

He explained the plot to me and, of course, neither of us knew at the time that it would some day make a list of the top one hundred movies of all time.

"Sounds like a classic, Frank."

"Yeah, right," he said, laughing. "Like a bum like me could make a classic film."

"What's the difference then?" I asked. "You entertain people. You make them happy with your movies, and your records."

"You're makin' me feel good, pally," he said, laughing again.

"How's it goin' with Juliet?"

He looked into his drink. "She's a sweet kid, but that's not gonna work out."

Great, I thought, now I had brought him down . . . again.

"And how's Ava?"

"Ava's Ava," he said. "Gorgeous, and maddening. Maybe I should just stick to hookers and show girls, Eddie."

"Frank—"

"Ya know, I think it's time for me to turn in," he said. "Thanks for listening, Eddie. You're aces, ya know that, kid?"

"I should be aces, Frank," I said, "I'm from Las Vegas."

Forty-two

IN THE MORNING WE had breakfast together and, before Jerry and I left, I called Fred Otash's office. I had to remind his girl who I was before she'd put me through.

"Mr. Gianelli," he answered without saying hello, "I tried to call you last night."

"I'm in Palm Springs."

"Miss Monroe?"

"Yes."

"Is she all right?"

"For now. Why were you lookin' for me? Any news?" I asked.

"No," he said, "just checking in, as I said I would. I have a couple of leads I'm going to follow up today. Will you be in later?"

"Should be back in a couple of hours."

"Good," he said. "I'll call you then."

I hung up, told Jerry it was time to leave.

"Hopefully," I said to Marilyn, "you'll be able to go home soon."

"I trust you, Eddie," she said, hugging me.

As we drove away I hoped that I would end up being worthy of that trust.

"You promised you'd do what?" Jerry asked.

"I told Marilyn I'd go and talk to Clark Gable's widow to see if she blamed Marilyn for Gable's death."

"And you think this woman is gonna agree to talk to you?"

"I don't know, Jerry," I said. "But I won't know until I ask. I hope she will."

"Well, better you than me," Jerry said.

"Yeah," I said, "what if Marilyn had looked at you with those big, beautiful eyes and begged you to help her?"

"Like I said," Jerry replied, "better you than me."

When we got on Highway 111 Jerry asked, "Where did Clark Gable live?"

"Encino," I said. "Marilyn gave me the address."

"When are we goin'?"

"I don't know," I said. "I told her I'd do it, I didn't say when."

As we got off 405 Jerry asked, "Where is Encino from here?"

"It's north, past Mulholland Drive. When we get to Ventura Boulevard, we'll be there. Probably won't take as long as it did to get from here to Palm Springs."

"We goin' now?"

"I'm a little tired of drivin', aren't you?"

"This car?" Jerry said. "Hey, I could drive it all day."

"Usually, I could, too," I said, "but right now I'm hungry and Otash is gonna give us a call later."

"There's a deli," Jerry said.

"A corned beef sandwich sounds good."

Jerry pulled over and we went inside. By the time we left we had two bags with sandwiches, fries and some cans of soda and beer. Within ten minutes we were sitting at the table in Marilyn's guesthouse.

"I wonder if anybody's been around here while we were gone?" he said.

"That'd be hard to know unless we were Daniel Boone and could read the ground."

"I was just wonderin'—I mean, if the main house is bugged."

"Well, either they'd have microphones in the house and a tape recorder nearby or maybe they'd have to come in and collect tapes."

"I could tell if someone jimmied a lock or a window," Jerry said.

"Why don't you take a look, then?" I suggested. "I'll wait by the phone."

"Want me to make some coffee first?"

"No," I said. "I'll have another cream soda." The beer was in the fridge for later.

"Okay," he said. "I'll get to it as soon as I finish my second sandwich. This ain't New York deli, but it ain't half bad."

"No, it isn't."

Forty-three

I SAT ON THE SOFA in the guesthouse, waiting for the phone to ring. I wasn't looking forward to driving to Encino to see Kay Gable. It had been many months since Clark's death, but that still didn't mean she would easily talk about it. And what if she did blame Marilyn? How would I tell Marilyn that?

The phone rang at that point, making me jump. At least I could stop thinking about Gable and Marilyn for a while.

"Mr. Gianelli?" Otash asked.

"Just call me Eddie," I said. "It'll be easier."

"Well, I don't know how much of this is going to be easy, Eddie."

"What do you mean?"

"We've got a dead body on our hands."

"What? Who?"

"That desk clerk," Otash said. "Max Johnson?"

"He's dead?"

"Yes."

"How?"

"He was strangled in his apartment."

"That dive we looked at?"

"No, his real apartment—at least, the one where he was sleeping."

"How did you find him?"

"I'm a detective, remember?"

"I'll need a little more than that, Mr. Otash."

"Call me Fred."

"You can explain the whole thing to me when I see you, Fred. I should move to a pay phone."

"We're not going to talk any state secrets here."

"Okay, what's next?"

"Well, I'm going to have to call that detective buddy of yours, Stanze."

"You haven't called the police yet?"

"No, I called you first, Mr.—Eddie. You're my client. My first duty is to you."

"Okay, so call Stanze," I said. "Will you be telling him that you called me?"

"Of course, and as soon as I tell him I'm working for you, he's going to want to see you."

"I'll be ready," I said.

"How are things going with Miss Monroe?"

"She'd like to come home."

"Well, in light of this I'd say she should wait a little while longer."

"I agree. Have you found out anything else?"

"When I located Mr. Johnson I thought he would lead me to your friend," Otash said. "It looks like I'll have to start all over again."

"From where?"

"That's the question," he said. "Look, Stanze will have you in after he talks to me. Might be tonight, might be tomorrow. We'll talk again after that."

"Okay."

"Meanwhile, watch your backs. Somebody out there is not afraid to kill."

"Thanks," I said. "I'll talk to you soon."

"Make sure you don't hold anything back from the police," he added.

"That'll be easy," I said. "I don't know anything."

When Jerry came back in he looked like he had something on his mind. I must have looked the same way.

"You go first, Mr. G."

"Let's step outside."

When we were behind the guesthouse I told him about Otash's call.

"I guess he must be pretty good if he found the guy," Jerry said. "Too bad he found him dead."

"Yeah," I agreed. "What'd you find?"

"Some gouges on the back door lock," Jerry said. "Somebody got in, or tried to get in."

"None on the front?"

"No."

"What about this building?"

"No, nothin' here."

"Those scratches weren't there before, Jerry?" I asked.

He looked embarrassed. "I can't say, Mr. G.," he replied. "I didn't look before."

"That's okay," I said.

I hadn't cleared the table yet. Jerry's cardboard container had one French fry left in it that he must have somehow missed. He snagged it, then started cleaning the table.

"What are we gonna do now?" he asked.

"I guess we better wait for Detective Stanze to call after he talks to Otash."

"What are we gonna tell 'im?"

"I don't know," I said. "Maybe we'll just wait for him to ask some questions, see what he wants to know. About the only thing I don't want to tell him is where Marilyn is."

We didn't even talk about that in the guesthouse, just in case.

Forty-four

Otash's guesstimate was pretty good.

We watched TV until late and the phone never rang. First thing in the morning, though, Stanze called.

"Gianelli? I think you and your buddy better come to my office this morning."

"What's it about?"

"Don't jerk my chain," Stanze said. "Just be here, quick."

I hung up and looked at Jerry, who had been getting ready to make something for breakfast.

"We're eatin' out."

We went to the West Los Angeles Station first. Stanze had not been the dick—in both senses of the word—that Las Vegas Detective Hargrove had been when we dealt with him, so I had no reason to want to jerk his chain. I wanted to cooperate.

"Here we are," I said, as an officer showed us in.

"That was quick," he said grudgingly. "I appreciate it. Have a seat."

We both sat down. He had an Italian takeout lunch in front of him and was using a plastic fork to eat it with.

"I hope you don't mind if I keep eating."

"Go ahead," I said.

"Looks good," Jerry said.

"It is," Stanze said. "Comes from a place around the corner, and they make sure I never find a hair in it."

"A hair?"

Stanze shivered. "Creeps me out."

"I don't blame ya," Jerry said.

"You can look at dead bodies, but you can't handle a hair in your food?"

Stanze glared at me and said, "It ain't the same thing!"

"Okay," I said, backing off.

He put the lid on his lunch and said, "Just talking about it creeps me out. I'll eat this later." He looked at us. "I understand you've retained Fred Otash."

"That's right," I said. "We needed somebody more familiar with the city."

Stanze looked directly at me. "I thought that was me."

"We wanted a little more help."

"What, specifically, did you ask Mr. Otash to do?"

"You must have asked him that."

"Now I'm asking you."

"I hired him to try and find Danny Bardini. What else am I here for?"

"You didn't hire him to do anything for Marilyn Monroe?"

"No."

"But she's still out of town?"

"Yes."

"And where were the two of you last night?" he asked.

"We were also out of town," I said.

"I'm gonna need a little more than that, Eddie," Stanze said.

"Are you telling me we need an alibi?"

"I'm working on a murder now," Stanze said. "Yes, you both need alibis."

Jerry looked at me and remained silent. He'd go along with anything I said.

"We stayed overnight at the home of Frank Sinatra," I said.

Stanze stared at me. "You're serious?"

"Why wouldn't I be?"

"Marilyn Monroe and Frank Sinatra. You travel in fast circles, Eddie."

"Part of my job."

"Nice work, if you can get it."

I remained silent.

"Okay, here's the deal," he said. "I've got a dead body, and I know you two have had contact with him. You think he had something to do with your friend's disappearance. So you found him, started to question him, something went wrong and he ended up dead." He pointed. "Maybe Big Jerry here doesn't know his own strength."

"Believe me, Detective," I said, "if there's anything Jerry knows it's his own strength. He'd never kill anyone . . . by accident."

"So then he meant to kill him."

"He didn't kill him at all," I said, "and neither did I."

"Then I'll need your alibis confirmed by Mr. Sinatra," Stanze said. "In person, no statements, or phone calls. The only statement I'll accept is one made in front of me."

"Mr. Sinatra is a very busy man," I said.

"I know, he's preparing for a visit from JFK," Stanze said. "I read the papers."

"Then you know he doesn't need his name connected to this."

"There's no reason for his name to be linked to anything unpleasant," Stanze said. "I just want him to come in and make his statement."

"If he comes anywhere near here it'll get in the papers," I said.

"What do you suggest?"

"That you come to Palm Springs with us to take his statement."

"Even if I go to Palm Springs," Stanze said, "I'll put your two asses in a cell to wait it out."

"No, you won't."

"Why not?"

"Because you're a detective," I said, "but you're not an asshole. You'd only do that to be a dick, because you've got no evidence to hold us on."

"If I go to Palm Springs I'm giving Mr. Sinatra preferential treatment."

"If he was a politician you'd be giving him preferential treatment," I said. "If the president was already staying with him you'd give him preferential treatment."

We were sitting with Stanze at his desk in the center of the squad room, not in his captain's office. I guess his boss was in that day. Stanze looked around, as if to see if anyone was listening in.

"I'm also gonna need a statement from Miss Monroe," he said.

"If you bring her in here it'll be a circus," I said. "She doesn't need that."

"Mr. Gianelli, I have a job to do. I can't be worried who gets involved in a media circus and who doesn't."

"Bullshit," I said, "it's done in Hollywood all the time."

"We're not quite Hollywood here."

"You're close enough."

He tapped his index finger on his desk while he did some thinking.

"I tell you what," he said. "I'll go to Palm Springs on one condition."

"What's that?"

"I get to interview both Frank Sinatra and Marilyn Monroe. Is she staying there with him?"

"I'll tell *you* what," I said. "I'll make sure Marilyn is in Palm Springs at Frank's house so you can take a statement from them both . . . if they agree."

"That doesn't tell me whether she's staying with him or not."

"No, it doesn't."

He studied me for a long moment.

"Okay," he said, "it's a deal."

"And I want *you* to do it," I said, "don't send those assholes from Palm Springs."

"No," he said, "I'll be doing this myself, with my partner. Set it up, and do it soon so you can keep your ass, and his, out of a cell."

"I'll set it up for tomorrow."

"Good."

I stood up.

"Can we go?"

"No, no," he said, waving at me, "we're not done yet. Sit back down."

Forty-five

I SAT BACK DOWN. Jerry had never moved.

"Fred Otash," Stanze said. "I want you to call him off."

"Why?"

"He's an ambulance chaser."

"He didn't chase us," I said. "We went to him."

"I'm still asking why."

"I understood there was no major case here that he'd be interfering with," I said. "I mean, all you were doing was looking for a missing person, right?"

"Not officially," he said. "I think I told you only a relative could report him missing. With all due respect to you claiming to be his . . . second cousin."

"Then why were you even looking?"

Stanze scanned the room.

"To be honest? Because the case involved Marilyn Monroe."

I pointed to him. "You don't act impressed," I said, "but you are. You're impressed with Marilyn Monroe."

"I'm not impressed," Stanze said, looking around again, "but like every other red-blooded male in America, she makes me horny as hell."

"Are you married?" I asked.

"No."

"So when you found out I was staying with her you were hoping to meet Marilyn?"

"Okay," Stanze said, looking embarrassed, "I admit that was the truth . . . before this became a murder case. But I do need a statement from her, and I'm willing to go to Palm Springs to get it, rather than make her come back here."

"Just to be nice."

"Don't let him kid you," Detective Bailey said, coming up behind his partner. He put both hands on Stanze's shoulders. "All he's been talkin' about since he met you is his meeting with Marilyn Monroe. You better believe he wants another helping."

"Dave—"

"Oops, sorry," Bailey said. "I've cracked the professional veneer."

I knew then who Stanze kept looking around for.

"Dave, I can fill you in later on what's going on," Stanze said.

"Sure, partner," Bailey said. "I can take a hint." He looked at us. "Gents."

"Guess I should've warned you he was comin' up behind you," I said. "Sorry."

"He's six months from retirement," Stanze said. "Every month he gets . . . worse."

"So he'd be going to Palm Springs with you?"

"Yes, but I'll do my best to keep his mouth shut."

I looked at Jerry, who still hadn't said a word.

"Okay," Stanze said, "so you're not going to terminate Fred Otash."

"He's the one who found that clerk," I said. "If he'd been

alive, maybe he would've found Danny, so no, I'm not gonna fire him."

"Then he better stay out of my way as far as the murder is concerned."

"He's gonna keep lookin' for Danny," I said.

Stanze looked at Jerry.

"You got anything to say?"

"Mr. G.'s doin' okay," Jerry said.

"Yeah," Stanze said. "Now we're done. Set up those statements for tomorrow."

I stood up. Jerry hesitated, and when Stanze didn't say anything else, he got up.

"I'll be in touch."

"I'll be waiting."

Jerry and I left the station.

In the car I said, "What do you think?"

"Dog and pony show," Jerry said.

"Too rehearsed, right?"

Jerry nodded.

"The partner's close to retirement, so he's supposed to be the comic relief."

"Stanze is just too damn friendly," Jerry said, "and the comment about Miss M. makin' him horny?"

"Just to make us think he's one of us boys."

"Right."

"So then why the trip to Palm Springs?" I asked.

"Maybe," Jerry said, "he's really a fan of Mr. S.'s."

"I guess that's possible," I said. "Damn, I hate to ask this of Frank."

"He'll do it," Jerry said.

"Oh, I know he'll do it," I said, "I just hate to ask."

Forty-six

WE STOPPED AT A pay phone. I laid my change out, inserted it and dialed Frank's number.

"Can Marilyn hear you?" I asked, when George put him on.

"No, she's outside. What's goin' on?"

"We're dealin' with a murder now."

"Whose?"

"The desk clerk in the motel where Danny was stayin'," I said, "only they claim he was never there."

"Maybe he wasn't."

"He's been wiped from their registration records, but he was there."

"What do you need from me?"

"To keep me and Jerry out of jail you need to make a statement that we were there with you last night."

"Where do I go to make this statement?"

"We'll bring the investigating detective to you," I said. "Him and his partner."

"When?"

"Tomorrow."

"Fine."

"Frank, I'm sorry I got you involved—"

"Hey, murder's murder, kid," he said. "I'll do what I can to keep you and Jerry out of jail."

"Well," I said, feeling bad at that moment, "maybe I overstated the case, but it would go a long way toward keepin' us from bein' suspects."

"It's okay, kid," Frank said. "Just bring 'em up tomorrow."

"We'll be there early, I'm sure," I said. "Frank, they want to take a statement from Marilyn, too. Only I didn't tell them she's stayin' with you. I only told them she'd be there tomorrow."

"I get it. You want to talk to her now?"

"Yeah, thanks."

He put the phone down and it was picked up moments later by Marilyn.

"Eddie? What's wrong?"

As gently as I could I told her that there'd been an unfortunate murder, that the police wanted statements from her and Frank to confirm Jerry's and my alibi.

"The police are coming here?" she asked, her voice quavering.

"Yes, they'll be comin' with us, tomorrow."

Her voice got calmer when she heard I'd be there.

"Okay, Eddie."

"They just need some things confirmed."

"Okay, Eddie," she said again. "I'll talk to them."

"It won't be hard to do," I said. "I think they're fans of yours."

"Really?"

Maybe, I thought.

"Really."

"You haven't found your friend yet?" she asked.

"No. We'll get you back home as soon as we can."

She lowered her voice then, and I knew Frank was nearby.

"Eddie, what about that . . . other thing?"

"I haven't had a chance to talk to Kay Gable yet, Marilyn," I said, "but I will. I promise."

"I know you will, Eddie."

"Let me talk to Frank again."

"Okay," she said, and handed the phone to him.

"Everything set?" he asked.

"Frank, try not to make it look like Marilyn is staying there," I said. "Tell George—"

"Don't worry, kid," Frank said, cutting me off, "we'll treat you all like guests."

"Okay, good," I said. "Thanks, Frank. Thanks a lot."

"Don't mention it, pally," he said. "I still owe you, remember?"

"Once we get Danny back it might even out."

"We'll see."

We hung up and I looked at Jerry.

"What now?" he asked.

I stepped out of the phone booth.

"I don't seem to be gettin' many good ideas," I said. "I might even think about going back to Vegas and leavin' this to Otash, except for one thing."

"Miss M."

"Right," I said. "She's become dependent on me, which is not a good thing for either of us. I mean, when this is over I'll be going back home. I'll just be another man who left her."

"It ain't like you guys are romantic or nothin'," Jerry said.

"No, but that might even make it worse," I said. "I mean, she's used to havin' romances break up."

"You thinkin' you're more like a father to her?" he asked.

"Nooo," I said with conviction. "It's like we said before, I'm more like a big brother at this point."

"She needs to start workin' again," Jerry said. "Maybe she'll be . . . better then."

"Yeah," I said, "maybe."

I picked up the phone, dropped in a dime, dialed Stanze's number and waited.

"Might as well get us set up for tomorrow now," I said. "This way we'll know what time we have to get up."

"Good," Jerry said, "when you're done with that we can talk about what's for dinner."

Forty-seven

STANZE AND HIS PARTNER showed up right on time at 9:00 A.M. We were waiting so we wouldn't have to let them in. Guess I was the one being a bit of a dick.

"You coming with us?" Stanze asked.

"No," I said, "you can follow us. We might not be returning the same time you are."

"You guys had breakfast?" Jerry asked.

"Just had time for coffee," Bailey said. "Why, you hungry?"

"He's always hungry," I said.

"So's he," Stanze said.

"Got a favorite place?" I asked. "We'll follow you there, then you can follow us to Palm Springs."

"Sounds like a deal to me," Bailey said.

"Me, too," Jerry said.

I had a feeling my partner and Stanze's partner were going to get along.

* * *

During breakfast the conversation was carried by Jerry and Detective Bailey. They had similar tastes in food, similar attitudes about it, and sort of got into an unofficial contest to see who could eat the most pancakes.

As Bailey pushed himself away from the table Stanze said, "I think you finally met your match, Dave."

"Oooh . . ." Bailey groaned.

Smiling, Jerry finished the last of his meal and stood up.

They walked ahead of us as we went to the cars.

"They're like two big kids," Stanze said.

"You and your partner should know, Stanze, that Jerry's not stupid."

"What makes you say that?"

"I don't know, just in case you're tryin' to run some kind of game on him."

"What kind of game?"

"Buddyin' up," I said. "Look, I'm just . . . warnin' you."

I sped up before Stanze could respond, passed Jerry and Bailey and got to the Caddy first.

We led the way to Palm Springs and I had pretty much the same conversation with Jerry along the way.

"Yeah, I kinda figured he was bein' a little too friendly," Jerry said.

"Then again, he is near retirement," I said.

"Don't make no difference," Jerry said. "Once a cop—always a cop."

"Yeah."

"I don't usually mix good with cops, but this one . . . he seems okay."

"So you don't think he's runnin' a game on you?"

Jerry shrugged.

"What's the difference? He ain't gonna get nothin' from me I don't wanna give 'im."

"Plus there's nothin' to give him anyway," I said.

"So let him run his game," Jerry said. "It was a hoot watching him try to eat all those pancakes."

"Bet he's sufferin' now," I said, and we both started laughing.

"Hope he pukes in his partner's lap," Jerry said while laughing.

I pointed and said, "Don't miss your turnoff."

Forty-eight

GEORGE CAME DOWN to meet us when we pulled into Frank's place. He must have gotten the construction guys to take the day off, or go to an early lunch. It was quiet as we got out of the cars.

"George Jacobs," I said, "these are Detectives Stanze and Bailey."

"How do you do," George said. "Mr. Sinatra is waiting by the pool. Follow me, please."

"Don't shit your pants when you meet him," Bailey said to Stanze in a stage whisper.

"Shut up, Dave."

We all followed George up the stairs to the pool. When Frank saw us coming he stood up. He was wearing an expensive-looking short-sleeved shirt, gray slacks and white boat shoes.

"Hey, Eddie," Frank said. "Jerry. How ya doin'?"

"We're doin' good, Frank," I said. "This is Detective Stanze, and his partner Detective Bailey."

"The gents who want my statement," Frank said. He extended his hand. "Welcome."

"It's a pleasure, Mr. Sinatra," Stanze said, almost stammering. "I—I have all your albums."

"All of 'em? That's a lot of vinyl, kid."

"Mr. Sinatra," Bailey said respectfully.

"Pull up a lounge chair. Anybody want a drink? Some coffee, maybe?"

"Coffee'd be good," Bailey said.

"Yes, fine," Stanze agreed.

"George, bring coffee all around," Frank said.

"Yes, sir."

Frank's valet went to get the coffee and we all grabbed lounge chairs. Everybody sat down but me.

"Frank, where's Marilyn?"

"She's inside, Eddie. Waitin' in the living room. I had George give her some tea when she got here."

"I'll go and sit with her," I said. "I don't want her gettin' nervous."

"Sure," Frank said. "I'll talk to the detective out here and then bring them inside."

"I've got a better idea," Stanze said. "Why don't I go with you, Eddie, and my partner can talk to Mr. Sinatra. If we work it this way we'll be out of here sooner."

"I don't want you scarin' her," I said.

And he didn't want me cooking up a story with her.

"I'll be real nice," Stanze said.

"Okay," I said, "okay, come on."

I looked at Jerry, who just nodded that he'd stay right where he was.

Marilyn saw us coming into the living room. On the coffee table in front of her was a tray with a china cup and teapot. She almost ran to me but when she saw Stanze she stopped herself.

"Marilyn," I said, "how're you doin'?"

"Okay, Eddie," she said.

"You remember Detective Stanze," I said.

"Miss Monroe," Stanze said. "It's a pleasure to see you again."

"Detective."

She was wearing what I had come to realize she always relaxed in—jeans and a sweatshirt.

"Can we sit down, Miss Monroe?" he asked. "I won't take long. I just need to ask a few questions."

"Of course, Detective," she said. "I want to be as helpful as I can."

They sat down. I was about to join them when Stanze looked up at me.

"Miss Monroe, do you suppose we could talk without Eddie in the room? Would that be okay?"

"Well . . ." She looked up at me and I nodded. "All right."

"We'll come out by the pool, Eddie, when we're done," Stanze said.

"Sure, Detective, sure."

I left the living room, but instead of going out by the pool I turned and went into the kitchen. George was putting the coffeepot and some cups on a tray.

"You need any help, George?"

"No, sir," George said, "but thank you."

"Sure."

"Don't you worry, Mr. Gianelli," George said, picking up the tray. "Mr. S. will only tell them what they need to know."

"That's all I want him to do, George," I said. "There isn't anythin' else to tell."

"Yes, sir," George said. "Whatever you say. You comin' out for coffee?"

"Yeah, George," I said, "I'll be there in a minute. Mind if I use the phone?"

"Go right ahead."

He left with the tray and I dialed Fred Otash's number. I

hadn't had a chance to talk to him the day before when we got back from the police station.

"Mr. Otash is not in at the moment, Mr. Gianelli," Leona said.

"Can I leave him a message?" I asked.

I heard her sigh heavily. What did she have against me anyway? "Oh, all right. What's the message?"

"Tell him we're out of town but will be back later today," I told her. "I'll call him as soon as we get back."

"You're out of town," she said, "and what?"

I repeated the message to her and she repeated it back as she wrote it down. Apparently, Fred Otash had not hired her for her secretarial skills.

"Okay," she said, "I got it, Mr. Gianelli."

"Thank you, Leona."

"My name's Miss Deeds, Mr. Gianelli," she said. "Please remember that."

"I will, Miss Deeds," I said, "I will."

Forty-nine

BY THE TIME I got out to the pool Frank, Jerry and Bailey were drinking coffee. The detective had apparently put his notebook away.

"Eddie," Frank called, "your coffee's going to get cold."

"Thanks, Frank."

I walked over and picked up the cup that had been poured for me.

"Am I interrupting?" I asked.

"No," Bailey said, "I finished up with my questions. We're talking about what a dick Burt Lancaster was on the set of *From Here to Eternity*."

"I never said that," Frank pointed out.

"Yeah, but you insinuated it."

"Jerry?"

"I didn't get that from what you said, Mr. S."

"Thank you. Hey, here's Marilyn."

I turned and saw Marilyn and Stanze walking toward us; they were both laughing. I could tell by the look on Stanze's face that he was in love with her, like every other man who'd ever seen her. She was even hanging on to his arm. The man who I thought might be playing us was now being expertly played by a woman who didn't even realize she was doing it. I wondered how dangerous Marilyn Monroe would be if she ever acquired some self-confidence.

"Coffee, Marilyn?" Frank asked.

"I had enough tea, Frank, thanks," she said, "but maybe Detective Stanze would like some?"

"No, thanks," Stanze said, "I think my partner and I have what we came for. We should stop bothering you folks. You have busy lives."

"That's very true," Frank said. "I have a commander in chief to prepare for."

"That's right," Stanze said. "I read that JFK was coming here. That must be very exciting."

"It is," Frank said.

"Come on, Dave," Stanze said. "Let's go."

They shook hands with Frank and Marilyn—Bailey stammering his name as he did so. I walked both detectives to their car.

"Our alibis check out?" I asked.

"For now," Stanze said. "And Miss Monroe supports your story."

"So while you're lookin' for the killer of the clerk, you'll be lookin' for Danny as well?"

"Yeah, Eddie," Stanze said, "we'll keep our eyes open for Danny. But tell your PI to stay out of our way. *Comprende?*"

"I think he knows how to do that," I said.

Stanze laughed. "Not if past history is any indication."

He and Bailey got in their car and drove away. I returned to the pool.

"How did we do?" Frank asked.

"Great," I said. "I think Jerry and I are off the hook . . . for now."

"Good," Frank said. "I'm gonna get my construction crew back here."

"Thanks, Frank."

"Sure, kid."

He went into the house, leaving Marilyn by the pool with me and Jerry.

"That detective was very nice," she said. "Nicer than the first time, and very young."

"He had stars in his eyes," I said.

"For Frank?" she asked.

"And you."

"He was sweet to me."

"Aren't men usually sweet to you, Miss M.?" Jerry asked.

"Not all of them, Jerry."

"Then the ones who ain't are jerks."

She smiled.

"And you're sweet, Big Jerry," she said, stroking his face. I'd never seen Jerry blush before.

Marilyn turned to me and asked, "Are you staying?"

"No. And we've been back and forth too many times already."

"What do you mean?"

"This time we're going to stay in L.A. until we find Danny, and until you're able to go home again."

"How long will that be, do you think?"

"I don't know, but at least now we've got the cops and a private eye working on it."

"That sounds like a lot," she said.

"Yeah, it does."

I only hoped it was enough.

✳　✳　✳

We said good-bye to Frank and Marilyn, telling them we'd see them again when it was all over.

"Stay in touch, Eddie," Marilyn said, "so I know you're safe."

"I'll call," I said. "I promise."

Fifty

WE DROVE BACK TO Brentwood and Marilyn's house. It seemed to be that was all we'd been doing, driving back and forth, accomplishing nothing.

As soon as we entered the guesthouse I phoned Fred Otash's office.

"Is he in, Miss Deeds?"

"Yes, he is, Mr. Gianelli," she replied politely. "Hold on, please."

She switched me over and Otash came on the line.

"Mr. Gianelli, I assume you're back?"

"Yes, we are."

"Good," he said. "May I drive out to see you?"

"Sure, when?"

"Now," he said. "I can be there in an hour. I have one other short stop to make."

"Okay, we'll be here. Pull into the drive and come to the guesthouse."

"The guesthouse, all right. I'll see you soon," he said, and hung up.

"Wonder if he's got any news for us?" Jerry said.

"I just hope nobody else is dead," I said. "Seems like every time we get together somebody—"

"Don't say it, Mr. G."

"Yeah, okay," I said. "It's just such a . . . coincidence."

"That's the word I didn't want you to say."

"We got any coffee to make when Otash gets here?" I asked.

"I can get some from the kitchen in the main house," he said. "I'll be right back."

But he didn't come right back. In fact, he didn't come back at all and I had to go looking for him.

"Jerry?" I called, entering the main house.

No answer.

"Crap." If he went missing like Danny . . . but he wasn't, so I didn't have to finish that thought. Instead, I had some new thoughts. When I entered the kitchen and saw him spread out on the floor, blood pooled around him, I feared the big guy was dead.

Fred Otash made good time, which meant he got there while the ambulance crew was still loading Jerry into the back.

"What happened?" he asked, coming up on me.

"He went into the main house and walked into somethin'," I said. "I don't know what happened because he's not conscious, but at least he's alive."

"That's good, that he's alive, but what's the diagnosis?"

"They have to get him to the hospital and see how bad the head injury is."

"What was he—"

"Look, can we talk on the way?" I said, cutting him off.

"They won't let me ride in the ambulance with him, but I'm going to the hospital."

"Okay, I'll drive," Otash said, "and I'll bring you back."

"No, I got a better idea. I'll drive myself. You go into the house and see what you can find. Figure somethin' out, Fred. Do your job."

Before he could respond I trotted over to the Caddy and got it started. He was still standing in the drive when I backed out and took off after the ambulance.

Fifty-one

THE CLOSEST HOSPITAL WAS in Antioch; it only took the ambulance seven minutes to get Jerry there. I was impressed. By the time I parked and got inside he was already in emergency.

"You'll have to wait out here, sir," a nurse told me, pointing to a waiting room.

I went and sat for ten minutes before I got up and found a phone. I called Dean's number in Beverly Hills. Jeannie said he was in New York but asked me what I needed. When I told her that Jerry was in the hospital she said she'd call their doctor and have him come right over there.

"I know Dean would want to help, Eddie," she said.

"Thanks, Jeannie."

I was still in the waiting room when Dean's doctor came walking in. I didn't know him, but somehow he picked me out.

"I'll get in there and see what's going on," he promised. "Sit tight."

I figured I had done everything I could, so I did just that.

* * *

Fred Otash showed up about an hour after Jerry had been brought in.

"How is he?" he asked.

"I don't know," I said. "They're workin' on him. I called Dean Martin and Jeannie sent over their doctor."

Otash sat next to me.

"What'd you find out?"

"Not much," he admitted. "Looks to me like Jerry must have had his head in the refrigerator when somebody came up behind and hit him."

"That's about the only way somebody would've been able to take him."

"Before I left, Detective Stanze arrived at the house," he told me. "He'll be in here soon."

"Fine," I said. "I'm not goin' anywhere."

Otash fell silent, but sat with me.

Twenty minutes after Otash arrived, Stanze walked in.

"How is he?" he asked.

"We're still waitin'," I said.

"Looks like somebody jimmied the back door more than once," Stanze said. "They must've been in there when Jerry came in. First he surprised them, then they surprised him. There was a lot of blood, but that's what happens with head wounds."

Stanze sat on the other side of me.

"What were you guys doing?" he asked.

"Fred had called and said, he was comin' over," I explained. "Jerry went into the main house to find some coffee. When he didn't come back I went lookin' for him, found him out cold on the floor."

"That's it?" Stanze asked.

"That's it, Detective," I said. "We weren't doin' anythin' but tryin' to make coffee."

Stanze nodded.

"You don't mind I'll stick around a while."

"I don't mind."

At that point his partner walked in with two bags filled with coffee containers.

"I didn't know who'd be here," he said, handing them out.

"Can't have too much coffee," Otash said.

Bailey nodded, sat down across from us, and put the other bag of coffees on the table next to him.

"You don't mind I'll stay a while," he said to me. "I kinda like the big lug."

"Sure."

We sat quietly and drank our coffee.

The emergency room doctor came out with Dean's doctor in tow an hour and a half after they brought Jerry in.

"He's got a hard head," he said. "He has a hairline fracture of the skull, and we had to drain some blood to take pressure off his brain."

"How do you do that?" I asked.

"We had to drill a hole in the skull to drain the blood out," the doctor said.

I heard a sharp intake of breath from somebody, probably Bailey.

"He has a fracture and you had to drill a hole?" I asked.

"That's right."

"How is he?"

"He's unconscious, but we're very optimistic."

"And what's that mean?"

"It means most people wake up within hours of an injury like this," the doctor said. "Some wake up . . . later."

"How much later?"

"Depends. Days, week, months . . ."

"Years?"

"Sometimes."

"Never?" I asked. "Is there a chance he might never wake up?"

"There's always that chance," the doctor said. "We should know more later tonight, or tomorrow."

"Doctor," Stanze said, showing his ID, "did he ever say a word? Anything?"

"Nothing," the doctor said.

Dean's doctor looked at me and said, "They've done all they can."

"Yeah," I said to both doctors, "thanks."

"Leave your information with the front desk," the emergency room doctor said, "including a number where we can get ahold of you."

"Yeah, okay."

The doctor turned and left.

"Eddie, we'll be back in the morning to see if he's awake and can make a statement," Stanze said.

"How about putting a man on his door, Stanze?" I asked. "I mean, somebody did try to kill him."

"Well, we don't know that for sure—the intent, I mean, but you're right. I'll put a uniform on his door."

"Okay, thanks. Give them my name and description, will you? I'll be comin' back."

"Yeah, I'll leave orders nobody gets in but you or Otash."

Bailey grabbed the bag of extra coffee. "You want me to leave these?"

"We're going to go out for coffee and something to eat," Otash said.

Bailey nodded.

He and Stanze left.

"Come on, Eddie," Otash said. "Let's leave your info and then go."

"Yeah, yeah," I said, "okay."

At the desk they took my number, and when I asked about making payment they said that Dean Martin's wife had called and all bills were to be sent to them.

"Your friend has friends in high places," the nurse said, smiling.

"Yeah," I said, "he does."

Otash took me by the arm. "Come on, Eddie."

I let him guide me outside.

Fifty-two

WE FOUND A DINER a few blocks away, pulled over and parked both cars. Inside the greasy smell of the place awakened the hunger in me. I kept thinking Jerry would want me to eat.

"You're probably used to better places to eat in Vegas," Otash said. "To tell you the truth I'm used to better, too, but every once in a while I just want some greasy diner food."

We sat in a cracked red-leather booth. A tired waitress came over and gave us menus.

"Bring me a beer," I told her.

"I'll have one, too," Otash said.

"Comin' up."

When she came back with two glasses of beer I ordered chicken in a basket and Otash ordered a burger platter.

"I'm sure Jerry'll be all right, Eddie," he said.

"He's got a hard head," I said. "He'll be okay. You know, I've seen him maybe four times in the past two years, and the big lug is probably one of the best friends I've got. Him and Danny. Whoever's behind this, they've done damage to my two best friends, and it's because they were both tryin' to help me."

"No point in feeling guilty about it," Otash said. "The best thing to do is find out who's behind it and make them pay."

"We've got to find Danny," I said. "Have you checked all the hospitals in town?"

"Hospitals, morgues, I've checked all the drunk tanks and jails in a hundred-mile radius. No sign of him."

"Then he's alive, unless he's out in the Pacific somewhere, weighed down."

"Look," Otash said, "I was coming over to discuss something with you. Are you prepared to listen? Or do you want to feel sorry for yourself all night?"

For a split second I felt a flash of anger and wanted to go over the table at him, but then it faded.

"I'm ready," I said.

He breathed a sigh of relief. "Good. For a minute there I thought you were going to jump me."

"For a minute there," I said, "so did I."

Our meals came and we both ate as if we hadn't eaten for days. I could still see my friend, Jerry, on the floor covered in blood, and yet I was ravenous. What did that say about me?

"Okay, Fred," I said, "what did you want to talk to us about?"

"I went back to that motel, talked to everybody—the owner, the front-desk clerks, and the maids."

"And none of them remembered Danny, right?"

"Wrong," he said. "One maid not only remembered Danny, she remembered letting you into his room."

"That's right," I said, "she dickered with me and let me in for a sawbuck, I think."

"Well, for a double sawbuck she told me that Danny had been there for one day and one night before he disappeared. She said they got his stuff out of there before the owner even knew he'd checked in. And she said she knew from the start that there was something fishy about that clerk, Johnson. When I told her he was dead, she didn't bat an eyelash."

"So what's it all mean?" I asked. "Did she give you anything helpful?"

"Yes."

"What?"

"A matchbook."

"A what?"

"She cleaned Danny's room after he disappeared. She kept everything."

"Why?"

"She said she figured the way he vanished somebody would come looking for him."

"So why didn't she offer me the matchbook?"

"She said she would have, if you'd come back," Otash said. "She was afraid you'd try to get it for the same sawbuck. She wanted you to come back and offer her more money."

"So where's the matchbook?"

Otash took it out of his pocket and set it down on the table. The cover had garish purple and yellow letters spelling out: THE LAVENDER ROOM.

"Strip club? Dance club?" I asked. "What?"

"I checked," Otash said. "It's a strip club—or gentlemen's club. Whatever you call it, it has naked women."

"So you think Danny left it behind?"

"I asked her what else was in the wastebasket and she said candy wrappers, chip bags, things from a vending machine and some soda cans he probably got from a convenience store down the road."

"Let me guess," I said. "The candy was Hershey's bars, the chips barbecue, and the soda cans Dr Pepper."

Otash took out his notebook, turned to the right page and read his notes. "You're right."

"That's Danny."

I knew how Danny liked to raid vending machines when he was in hotels or motels. He ate the stuff not only in the room, but when he was on a stakeout. And Hershey's were his favorite.

"So his clothes weren't left behind and stored by the motel?"

"No," Otash said, "personal things were gone."

"Did she see who took Danny? Or who took his things?" I asked.

"She saw two men come and clean the motel room out."

"Did she describe them?"

"Well enough. She's very observant. A burly, curly-haired guy and a man with a scar on his forehead."

"So she just saw them clean the room out, right? Didn't see them take Danny?"

"No, he wasn't taken from the motel."

"Maybe he went to this club and was taken from there."

"That's what I think," Otash said. "I'm going to check it out tonight."

"*We're* gonna check it out tonight," I said. "I'm goin' with you."

"I thought you might say that."

"Don't argue with me."

"I won't," he said. "I'm going to change my clothes. I'll stand out like a sore thumb in this suit. I'll stop by here and pick you up."

"Come to the hospital," I said. "I'll be there, waiting to hear something about Jerry."

"Okay," Otash said. "Do you have a gun?"

"Jerry's is in the guesthouse," I said.

"Have you ever used one?"

"Yeah, in the army. A forty-five, like Jerry's."

"Considering what's been going on, you better bring it."

"It's gonna be bad news if the cops catch me with it," I pointed out.

"It might be even worse news," Otash said, "if we run into trouble and you get caught without it."

"Okay, but I won't carry it into the hospital. I'll put it in the trunk, where Jerry stashes it."

"Good," Otash said. "We can pick it up before we go to the Lavender Room."

"This may be a silly question, but you'll have a gun, too, right?"

He nodded. "My thirty-eight."

"Good," I said. "We'd be in trouble if I was the only one armed."

Fifty-three

I WENT BACK TO THE GUESTHOUSE after cleaning the kitchen floor in the main house. I didn't want Marilyn finding blood all over the kitchen. That would really do a number on her.

I showered, changed and got Jerry's gun from where I'd left it in a kitchen drawer. When the cops had been called, after I'd found Jerry, I'd removed his gun so they wouldn't see it and keep it.

Cops, I thought. Stanze and Bailey had me confused. They had seemed genuinely concerned about Jerry at the hospital. Were they still running a game on us, or had they never been running a game at all? Dealing with that prick Hargrove in Las Vegas had given me a bad opinion of detectives.

I was about to leave for the hospital—Jerry's gun uncomfortably in my belt—when I realized I hadn't talked to Jack Entratter in a while. He was going to be pissed that I hadn't called him.

I didn't really want to deal with him at this point, but better to make contact and get it over with than to let any more time go by.

I dialed Jack's number, got past his girl and listened for a few minutes while he chewed me out for not staying in touch.

"Okay," he said, sounding spent, "now that I got that out of the way, what's goin' on?"

I gave him the whole story, tossing in Frank's and Dean's names liberally. As long as he thought I was working for or with his buddies, he wouldn't bitch too much about my absence. When I got to the part about not having found Danny yet, and Jerry being in the hospital, he commiserated.

"I'm sorry about your friends, Eddie, but it doesn't sound like you've gotten anywhere since you went to L.A."

"No, but that may change." I told him about the matchbook cover.

"I'm gonna check on the Lavender Club, see if we know who's runnin' it," he said. I knew who he meant when he said "we." I didn't bother saying I thought Otash could handle that. Instead I just said thanks, and told him I'd stay in touch.

"Call me if you need anything," he said, "like your ass bailed out."

"Thanks, Jack."

I hung up and went out to the Caddy. I opened the trunk, took the gun from my belt and stuck it in the wheel well, where Jerry had put it before. I was fine as long as the cops didn't search my car.

I closed the trunk and drove to the hospital.

"He's not awake yet," the doctor said. He was the emergency room doctor who had worked on Jerry. I hadn't noticed much about him earlier, but now saw that he was young, probably in his early thirties. He had an air of both confidence and competence about him.

"I warned you," he went on, "so far we're not looking at this as anything unusual."

"I understand," I said. "I was just hopin'. Where is he?"

"We've put him in a room."

"A private room?"

"Yes," he said, "apparently Mrs. Dean Martin insisted on that."

"Good. Can I see him?"

"He won't know you're there."

"I know, I just want to see him."

"Sure."

The doctor walked me to the room and left me there. I nod-ded to the cop guarding the door as I went in. Jerry was a big lump on the bed, his head swathed in bandages. He looked pale, but while most people looked frail in hospital beds, he still looked healthy and burly.

I walked up closer to the bed and looked down at him.

"Sorry, big guy," I said. "You took the brunt of it, this time. I'm gonna find out who clobbered you and make 'em pay. You can count on it."

He didn't blink.

I leaned closer and lowered my voice.

"Oh yeah, I'm gonna borrow your forty-five," I said. "I hope you don't mind."

I could almost hear him thinkin', *Hell no, Mr. G. Go ahead. Just don't lose it.*

"Yeah, I'm gonna make 'em pay," I said, "as long as I don't shoot myself in the foot."

When I came out into the waiting room Fred Otash was there, wearing jeans and a windbreaker.

"How's he doing?"

"Not awake, no change," I said. "They're sayin' it's not un-usual."

"You ready to go look at some naked babes?"

"Sure."

"You got that item we talked about?"

"In the trunk."

"Well, let's get it out of the trunk, and get going," he suggested.

Fifty-four

WE WENT IN BOTH CARS, in case we wanted to split up.
After we pulled into the parking of the neon-lit Lavender Club I
joined him in his car and asked, "How good are your descriptions."

"Right down to a scar down the center of one of their foreheads," Otash said. "If they're here, we'll spot them."

We got out of the car. Once again the gun felt awkward in
my belt, like it was either going to fall out, or yank my pants
down. I wondered aloud if I shouldn't put it in my jacket
pocket.

"It'll get caught when you're trying to pull it out," Otash
said. "Also, it'll yank down the jacket so that someone will
know you've got something in there. Keep it in your belt."

I nodded my agreement.

We went in the front door and I blinked as the sheer volume
of lavender neon hit me.

"Jesus," Otash said, "this'll take some getting used to."

He was right, it was hard to see at first, and I wondered
why the management wouldn't realize that. As we got deeper

into the place, though, the neon faded. It got darker, easier to see the girls spotlit up on the stages. Most of them were already nude, it was strange how some of them looked more nude than others.

We found two seats, sat down and ordered beer. Otash turned his attention to the stage, where a woman with very large breasts was hanging upside down from a pole.

I was scanning the audience. The place was only about half full.

"Fred," I said, "we're supposed to be lookin' for these guys, remember? And they're not gonna be up on stage."

"Give me a break," Otash said. "I'm a busy man and I don't get out much. I don't live in Vegas, where this kind of thing is everywhere."

"It's not everywhere," I said. "It's in the clubs, just like here, and sometimes up on stage."

"Just look for that big scar right down the center of his forehead," Otash said. "That can't be very common."

"And the guy with him?"

"Burly, she said," Otash answered. "With curly hair. And when she saw them they were both wearing suits and ties."

"Well," I said, "if they wear suits and ties in here that'll make 'em stand out for sure."

The girl with the big tits got off the pole and was right side up, her breasts returning to their normal position.

Otash took a deep breath and looked at me.

"Who owns this place?" I asked. "Do you know?"

"The owner of record is some corporation. It's managed by a man named Sam Kearny."

"Do you know anything about him?"

"No," Otash said, "he could just be a name on a piece of paper."

I remembered Jack Entratter saying he was going to have someone look into who owned the place. Maybe he was able to get behind the corporate name. I'd have to call him later and find out.

We sat there for two hours, had two more beers, watched the girls rotate in and out until the one with the really big boobs waved at Otash because she was used to seeing him there by then.

When a new batch of girls showed, Otash leaned over to me and said, "I guess we should call it a night. We could try again tomorrow."

We started to get up when I grabbed his arm and pushed him back down.

"What?"

"Guy in a suit just came in," I said, jerking my chin toward the door.

The man stood bathed in purple while his eyes adjusted to the neon. He didn't have a scar, but was burly and had curly hair, albeit closely cut.

"He's alone," Otash said.

We watched him. Eventually, he turned, walked along the front wall and entered what was probably an office. The girls had been coming in and out through a pair of swinging doors, so we didn't think he was going backstage.

"He belongs here," I said.

"Or he knows the owner."

"We have to get back there," I said. "Danny may be in this building."

"Yeah, okay," he said. "You stay here in case I get into trouble."

"I'll come with you," I said.

This time he put his hand on my shoulder and pushed me down.

"That'd be too obvious. Just stay here and watch my back—but at the same time, be careful about pulling that gun."

"Right."

Jerry's .45 felt like it weighed fifty pounds. I sat back and watched Otash mosey across the room toward that doorway. Just as he reached it the door opened and a big, broad bouncer came walking out. He spotted Otash, put out a hand that sparkled with a couple of diamond rings and laid it on Otash's chest. They exchanged some words, and the bouncer pointed toward the front door. When we first came in I had noticed the restrooms, so Otash was either being shown out, or directed to the men's room. He started that way, with the bouncer right behind him. Briefly, he caught my eye, looking helpless.

I didn't waste any time. I got out of my chair and quickly crossed the room to that doorway. Yanking the door open I quickly slipped inside.

Fifty-five

I CLOSED THE DOOR behind me, found myself in a hallway. Voices were coming from a room at the end of the hall that was obviously an office, its door open. If anybody came out of that room, I'd be screwed. I'd have to claim I was looking for the men's room and see what happened.

The voices were simply a buzz. I had to get closer to hear what was being said. I wondered if the bouncer who had walked Otash out would come back and catch me from behind. I had Otash's last word in my head, about not drawing the gun. If I'd paused to think, I probably would not have rushed across the room in the first place and through this doorway, but the decision had been made so I had to come out of it with something.

As I crept down the hall toward the open door I passed several other doorways. I checked them quickly, hoping none of them would creak. Two closets, a bathroom, and a stairway heading down. I was tempted to go see if Danny was being held down there, but I decided to try to hear some of the conversation first. In fact, I could already hear some of it.

As soon as the voices became clear enough I stopped.

"In the hospital, still hasn't woke up," one voice said.

"Well, he better wake up," a second said. "They're not gonna like it if a homicide investigation gets started."

"There's already a homicide investigation, remember? Johnson?"

"Nobody cares about Johnson, but this guy got hit in Monroe's house. That's news."

"Don't worry about it," the first man said.

Apparently there were only two men in the room. I wondered if one of them had a scar down the center of his forehead. I could hear, but I couldn't see. For that I'd have to get even closer. Most of the room was out of sight. But getting closer would put me in a totally defenseless position if someone entered the hall from the other end.

"Where the hell is your partner?" the second man asked.

"Still at the hospital," the first man said. "He's keepin' an eye out."

"For what?"

"Whatever," the first man said. "A chance to finish the guy, news that he died, whatever."

"Do they know about that? Jesus, you're gonna kill a guy in the hospital? You know, you freelancers kill me."

"Yeah," the first man said, "that could be arranged."

"Very funny. Why don't you go out and look at some of the girls? Let me get back to work."

"I was just checking in for orders."

I heard a chair creak, and then the sound of somebody walking. I turned to hotfoot it back up the hall, but at that moment the door at that end started to open. I was seconds from being discovered from both ends. Use my bathroom story, or duck behind one of those other doors?

I made up my mind quickly, opened a door and stepped in, closing it behind me as gently as I could.

Fifty-six

IT WAS DARK AND I almost took a header down the stairs. I caught myself at the last second, then stood there quietly as the two men met in the hallway.

"Leavin' already, Harris?"

"Gonna check out some of the girls."

"You wanna go home with one just let me know," the bouncer said. "I got a few of 'em on a string."

Harris said, "I'm sure the feds would be happy to know they got a string of whores bein' run out of here."

Both men laughed and kept going in their respective directions. I waited a few more moments, then opened the door to peer out. That was taking a chance, because I could only see one way, up the hall toward the club. I opened it a little more, stuck my head out further and looked at the office door, which the bouncer had closed behind him.

This was my chance to get out of there, but I hesitated and looked behind me. The light from the hall illuminated the basement stairs. If there was the slightest chance that Danny was being held down there, I had to take it.

I closed the door and stood there long enough for my eyes to adjust to the dark. Enough light came from beneath the door to allow me to see the stairs. I started down, taking my time since I had no idea how many steps there were.

I wondered what had happened to Otash. Had he been kicked out of the place? Was he waiting for me outside? Or was he still inside?

I kept going down the stairs one at a time, keeping my hand on the wall because there was no banister. The stairs creaked, but I didn't think anyone upstairs could hear them.

Finally, I got to the bottom, wishing I had a flashlight. I looked around for a light switch. I didn't find one.

I started swatting the air, looking for a pull string attached to a lightbulb. I found one and grabbed it.

I looked up the steps. From my vantage point I could not see the light under the door. I wondered if anyone on the other side could see my light.

I pulled down on the string, intending to snap the light on for a second or two, just to get a look around. As the bulb came on it bathed the room in yellow light. I always hated yellow bulbs, and this one was about forty watts. By the dim light I saw a wooden chair in the center of the room. There were some stains on the floor in front of and next to the chair. In the yellow light I couldn't be sure, but I thought it was blood. Was it Danny's blood? There wasn't a lot of it, not as much as if someone had had their throat cut. But somebody had definitely been hurt.

I realized I'd left the light on too long, so I yanked on the string—and it snapped, leaving the light on. I dropped the string onto the floor, and tried to reach the small part that was still hanging from the light, but it was too high. I thought about using the chair to stand on, but the idea that it might have some of Danny's blood on it kept me from doing it.

Instead, I began to look for a way out. I just hoped somebody would think they had left the light on.

I found a door in another part of the basement. It was a loading double door, and I hoped it wasn't locked from the outside. It wasn't. I was able to open one side, go up the stairs, and then close the door without dropping it. The metal would have rang out loud and clear.

I looked around quickly. I was behind the building. I worked my way around to the front and found Otash sitting in his car. When I knocked on the window he just about jumped out of his skin.

I opened the passenger door. "Did that guy come out?"

"Yeah. I would have followed him, but I was worried about you," he explained. "I did get his plate number, though."

"Good. Let's get out of here. I'll meet you back at the hospital."

"What the hell happened—"

"Later," I said, getting out of his car. "The hospital."

"But why?" he asked. "Why don't we go back to Miss Monroe's, or somewhere—"

"Otash!"

"What?"

"The hospital!"

"Okay," he said, "okay, the hospital."

He started his engine and backed up. I ran to my Caddy, got in, fired her up and got out of there.

Danny had been in that basement. I felt it in my bones. But at that moment I was intent on getting back to the hospital to make sure Jerry was all right.

Fifty-seven

WHEN WE GOT TO THE HOSPITAL parking lot I got out of the Caddy and ran to Otash's car.

"Come on, we've got to get inside."

"What's going on?"

"I'll tell you on the way!"

While we ran into the hospital I tried to tell him what I found in the basement. He wasn't following me, so I said, "Somebody's going to make another try at Jerry."

We ran past the front desk, the nurse shouting after us. Jerry was on the second floor. Instead of waiting for the elevator I took the stairs adjacent to them. When we got to the second floor I led the way to Jerry's room. Nobody was on duty in front of it.

"There's no cop on the door!" I shouted.

I drew Jerry's gun and ran into his room. There was a cop in uniform standing next to his bed, looking down at him. I started for him with Jerry's gun, but Otash grabbed me from behind and pulled my gun hand behind my back as the policeman turned to look at us.

"Can I help you gents?" he asked.

"Yes, Officer," Otash said, "I'm Fred Otash and this is Eddie Gianelli."

"Yes, sir," the cop said, turning to face us. His hands were empty. The part of his forehead I could see beneath his cap brim was smooth and unscarred. "They told me you were allowed in the room. Is something wrong?"

"We heard something tonight that led us to believe this man is in danger."

"Here? In the hospital?"

"Yes, sir," Otash said. "I suggest you call for backup."

"I'll have to check that with my watch commander, sir."

"That's okay, son," Otash said, "and you better check with Detective Stanze, as well."

"Yes, sir."

As the cop left the room, I turned so the gun was still behind me. When he was gone I returned the gun to the back of my belt.

Otash turned on me and said, "I told you about that gun! You almost pointed it at a cop!"

"I know, I'm sorry," I said. "And thanks for stopping me."

"We'll have to stay here while he's checking on backup," Otash said.

"I wonder why he was in here and not out in the hall?" I said.

"There was no scar on his forehead," Otash said. "But still . . ."

"Where are you going?" I asked.

"I want to see where he went."

I stayed at Jerry's bedside until Otash returned. During that time the big guy didn't move or make a sound. I wasn't used to Jerry being so silent and still. It was unsettling.

When Otash came back in he said, "The cop's on the level. He radioed for backup and then used the phone to call Stanze."

"Still, what was he doin' in here?" I asked.

"When Stanze gets here," Otash said, "ask him to ask the cop. Meanwhile"—he lowered his voice—"why don't you go out to your car and stash that gun before the room is crawling with cops."

"That's a good idea."

When I left, Otash was at Jerry's bedside while the cop had returned to the door.

Stanze made good time, arrived just before the extra officers did.

"What's going on, Eddie?" he demanded.

"I have information that someone might try for Jerry again while he's in the hospital."

"And where did you get this information?"

"I'd rather not say, but I'm sure what I heard was legit."

"So you're asking me to act on information you overheard somewhere?"

"That's exactly what I'm askin' you to do."

Stanze shook his head slowly. "You're pushing it, Eddie."

"I haven't even started," I said.

I told him about finding the cop in Jerry's room, and wondering what he was doing there.

"I'll ask him," he said, "but I've known Officer Chester for five years. He's legit."

"Okay," I said, "if you vouch for him, that's okay with me."

Stanze hesitated, then said, "I'll ask him anyway."

Fifty-eight

STANZE HAD A HALF a dozen officers search the hospital for a man with a scar on his forehead. Then he sat me down and convinced me to tell him what I had done. I told him about the matchbook cover, the strip club, the conversation I had heard in the back office, and what I'd seen in the basement.

"You know, your PI should've told you to come to me with the matchbook," Stanze said. "We might have been able to do something. As of now I can't get a warrant to go into that strip club. I have no probable cause."

"Isn't what I'm tellin' you probable cause?" I asked.

"No, it's not enough to move on," Stanze told me. "All I can do is watch the strip club."

"Well, if Danny was there and they moved him, what are the chances they'll bring him back?"

"Probably slim."

"So then what good does it do for you to watch the place?"

"It's all you've left me," Stanze said. "I'll check out who owns it, and who runs it, but beyond that . . ."

"What about talkin' to the maid?"

"I can do that, but for all we know she gave Otash a random matchbook and a line of crap for his twenty bucks."

"Not after what I heard."

Stanze gritted his teeth and whatever he was thinking about saying to me never made it past his lips. He stopped himself, blew out a frustrated sigh and finally said, "I'm going to check with my officers."

We were in the hall outside Jerry's room. When he left I went back in. Otash gave me a look.

"He can't do anything," I said.

"No probable cause," Otash said, nodding.

"You knew that?"

"Of course."

"Then why did we go into that joint? Why didn't we just call Stanze to begin with?"

"Because," Otash said, "he would've said the same thing. He never would've gone inside. By the way, that was a big chance you took. I was trying to send you a message to stay put."

"I was never very good at reading sign language, or body language," I said. "I acted by instinct."

"Impulse, is more like it."

"Whatever," I said, "now we've got some information we can't do anything about."

"I'm going to check deeper into the Lavender Club's ownership."

"That's what Stanze said he was going to do."

"Good, the more the merrier," he said. "You going to stay here?"

"For now, yes."

"There's not much we can do at this time of night," he said. "I'm going to go home and get some shut-eye, get into my office early and start running down the club's owners."

"If you don't find me here, I'll be at the guesthouse."

"Okay," Otash said. He lowered his voice and put his hand on my arm. "Leave that gun where it is."

"Yeah, okay."

Otash left and I sat with Jerry for a while. Not only were Otash and Stanze running down the ownership of the club, but so was Jack Entratter. I had a feeling that Jack's contacts might be able to go deeper than the other two. I was going to call him first thing in the morning.

I sat in a chair next to Jerry's bed and dozed off.

I woke up to find Stanze shaking me.

"We haven't found anybody in the building matching that description," he said, "although the only thing you gave us is a scar on some guy's forehead."

"It's supposed to be very noticeable," I said, stretching.

"I'm leaving three officers here," he said. "One downstairs, one out by the desk on this floor and one in front of the door."

"I'm gonna stay all night, too."

"I'll tell them at the nurse's station, so they don't try to kick you out."

"Good, thanks."

"I'll give you a call tomorrow, Eddie," Detective Stanze said. "Meanwhile, try not to do anything else stupid, huh?"

"I'll give it my best shot."

Stanze stared at me for a long minute. "Stand up," he said.

"What for?"

"I want to see if you're doing something stupid right now . . . like carrying a piece."

"I don't have a gun on me, Detective," I said.

"Humor me. Stand up."

I stood up and he patted me down.

"Satisfied?"

"For now," he said. "I should search your car, but . . ."

I took my car keys out of my pocket and tried a monumental bluff.

"Here ya go," I said, holding the keys out to him.

"Never mind," he said, as the keys dangled from my fingers. "Just stay out of trouble."

"I'll do my best."

"Make sure that's good enough."

As Stanze left I sat back down with a sigh of relief. I was thankful Otash had told me to stash the gun in the car, and even more thankful that Stanze had not called my bluff.

"You gotta wake up, big guy," I said to Jerry. "I think I'm floundering more without you than I was with you."

If he heard me he wasn't giving any sign. I sat back in the chair, folded my arms and closed my eyes again.

Fifty-nine

I WOKE IN THE MIDDLE of the night and listened to the silence. It was too quiet. I sat up quickly, the only light coming in from the hall. I stood up and walked to the doorway. Where there was supposed to be a cop there was nobody.

I went back to Jerry's bed, located his buzzer to call the nurse and pressed it. I had to press it a second and third time before someone came—a middle-aged nurse who looked as if she, too, had just woken up.

"Oh," she said, "for a moment I thought your friend pressed the call button."

"Can you tell me what happened to the cop who was on the door to this room?"

"I can tell you what happened to all three of them," she said. "They were called back to their station."

"Why?"

"I was only told that they had to leave."

"And nobody thought to tell me?"

"Excuse me, sir, but I don't work for you," she said stiffly.

"Okay, look—what's your name?"

"Nurse Collins, sir."

"Miss Collins, I'm sorry about the way that came out," I said, "but this man is in danger and, frankly, if he's in danger so are you and the other nurses."

She frowned. "I hadn't thought of it that way. They said not to disturb you, but to tell you about it when you did wake."

"I see."

"What are we supposed to do?"

"I'm gonna stay all night," I said. "Just keep an eye out for strangers."

"Yes, sir."

"And if I have any trouble I'll press the call button and you come running with some orderlies."

"All right, sir."

"Big ones, if you have any."

"I'll find 'em," she promised.

I walked her to the door.

"I'm gonna close this door. If you or a doctor want to come in I'd appreciate it if you'd knock."

"I'll see to it."

"Tomorrow I'm gonna get us some help."

"Good," she said, "because I'm on duty again tomorrow night."

She returned to her station and I returned to mine. I was determined to stay awake, but you know what they say about the best laid plans . . .

I woke with a start, the sun streaming in the window directly into my eyes. I checked the time: 8:15 A.M. I picked up the phone and dialed the operator.

"Operator," a woman's voice said.

"Can I make a long distance call from here?" I asked.

"I'm sorry, sir, no," she said, "but there are pay phones in the lobby."

"What number do I dial to get the nurse's station on the second floor?"

"If you're in a room, sir, just press your call button. A nurse will respond immediately."

"Yeah, see, the problem is your idea of immediately and mine are two different things. What number can I dial to get the station?"

She told me, and I dialed it.

"Second-floor nurse's station," a woman said.

"Nurse Collins?"

"Yes."

"This is Eddie Gianelli, down the hall in Jerry Epstein's room?"

"Yes, Mr. Gianelli. Is your call button out of order?" she asked.

"I didn't try it. I preferred to call you this way. I need to go down to the lobby to make a long distance call."

"You can make it from your room, sir," she said, "but it will show up on your final bill."

"That's no problem," I said. "The operator told me I couldn't do it."

"I'll call her and arrange it, sir. She'll ring you when she has a line open."

"Okay, thanks."

I only had to wait ten minutes and then the phone rang. I grabbed it on the first ring, then realized how silly I was being. The phone was not going to wake Jerry up, although I wished it would.

"Yes?"

"You have a line, sir. You may dial your call."

"Thank you."

I dialed the Sands, Jack Entratter's office. He answered his own phone, which he does when his girl is out, or away from her desk.

"Eddie, where the hell are you? I've been tryin' to get you—"

"I'm at the hospital, Jack," I said. "Listen, did you look into the Lavender Club like you said you were?"

"I did, and you're in trouble, my friend."

"What kind of trouble? How bad?"

"The fed kind."

"You know, I thought I heard they were involved, but at the time I convinced myself I was wrong."

"Involved? Hell, they run it, Eddie. And do you know who owns the Lavender Club?"

"Who?"

"J. fucking Edgar Hoover, that's who," he said. "You're banging heads with the FBI, my friend."

Sixty

AFTER I HUNG UP on Entratter I called Otash's office and left a message with Miss Deeds to have him come right over to the hospital.

While I waited for Otash to arrive—or maybe even Stanze—I looked at Jerry, lying helpless in that bed, and realized that I had always thought of him as indestructible. Seeing him unconscious and unable to defend himself was kind of scary. But it also showed that anybody can be taken down if you take them from behind.

Otash arrived and looked disturbed—rested, but disturbed.

"What's going on?" he asked. "I haven't had a chance to make my calls yet."

"To check on the Lavender Club?"

"Well, yeah, that's what I was going to do."

"You don't have to."

"Why not?"

"I got the information already."

"From who?"

"Jack Entratter, my boss at the Sands."

"I've heard of Entratter," Otash said. "So what did he do, use the Sicilian pipeline?"

"Whatever he used, he got the info, and I don't think you would have gotten it. I don't even think the L.A. cops would've found it."

"What is it, top secret?"

"You might say that."

"Okay, don't keep me in suspense. Who owns the damned club?"

"You're gonna laugh," I said. "The owner of record is something called the JEH Group, Inc."

"JEH? What does that stand for?"

"This is the part you're gonna find funny," I said. "JEH stands for J. Edgar Hoover."

"What? Are you telling me that club is owned by the FBI?"

"That's what I'm tellin' you."

"Wait a minute—JEH? That's just stupid."

"All the more reason to believe it," I said. "Somebody just couldn't help but get cute about it."

"Jesus . . ."

"And did you notice anythin' odd when you came in?" I asked.

"Yeah, I did," he said. "No cops."

"Right," I said. "They were pulled in the middle of the night."

"You think the FBI had something to do with that, too?" he asked.

"I'd make book on it."

"This makes sense out of the conversation you heard in the club," he said.

"Yeah, but I don't think Harris and the guy with the scar are FBI. I think they're freelancers."

"Being paid by the feebs."

"Right."

"You know, if the FBI pulled the cops they're not coming back any time soon."

"I know," I said. "That's why I've made other arrangements."

"Also through Entratter?"

"Yes," I said. "Someone's got to keep Jerry safe while we run down these two guys. One of the calls you were gonna make was to run that plate number."

"Yes," he said, "I'm having Leona do it now."

"Good. If I'm right the car will be registered to the JEH Group. Maybe there'll be an address."

"Most likely a PO box."

"If it is we're screwed again."

"No, we're not. We'll just stake out the place and wait for one of them to show up, and this time we'll follow him."

"What if they realize someone left the light on in the basement?"

"Maybe nobody's been down there since, but it won't matter. They'll each blame somebody else."

"So Fred, are you sure you're willing to go against the FBI?"

"If you're right and these are freelancers who jumped the gun," he reasoned, "grabbed Danny and slugged Jerry, then we're not going against the whole FBI, just these two guys. I mean, the only reason the FBI would employ freelancers is deniability."

"That's one way of looking at it," I said.

"When are your other arrangements supposed to arrive?" he asked.

"Any minute. They'll watch Jerry in shifts until I tell them it's over."

"This," he said, "ought to be interesting."

He was right, it was.

Two guys arrived wearing suits and ties and iron under their arms. Young, dark-haired, pale and bored-looking, almost identical.

"You Gianelli?" one of them asked. "The one they call Eddie G?"

"That's me," I said, and even to myself I sounded like a bad Edward G. Robinson impersonator. "I'm Eddie Gianelli."

"I'm Vince, this is Bobbo," Vince said. "Mr. Roselli sent us."

"Johnny Roselli?" Otash asked.

"You know another one?" Vince asked.

I'd met Roselli one time. He ran L.A. and Vegas for Sam Giancana and his group. Entratter had said he'd call Roselli and get me some help looking out for Jerry.

"Dis da guy?" the other man asked. "Jeez, he's a big one. How'd they take him down?"

"From behind," I said.

He looked at his partner and said, "Ain't dat always da way?"

"Shut up, Bobbo," Vince said. He looked at me. "We'll be here for six hours and then we'll be relieved. Mr. Roselli says you should go and do what you gotta do. Him and Mr. Entratter made all the arrangements, and Mr. Roselli made a promise."

"The cops were supposed to be here watchin' him," I said.

"That figures," Vince said.

"Well, they may be back."

"That's okay," Vince said, "we get along good with cops. They understand cash."

"Okay, Vince," I said. "Just make sure nothin' happens to him."

"Hey," Vince said, "Mr. Roselli makes a promise, we keep it. That's our job, and we're good at it."

"Hey," Bobbo said, "is it true you're friends with Frank and Dean?"

"Yeah, it's true."

"Jeez, dem guys is great."

"I tell you what," I said. "You do your job, and I'll get you free tickets next time they're in Vegas. And a comped room at the Sands."

"Really?" Bobbo asked. "Jeez, thanks, Mr. Gianelli."

"We'll do our job either way," Vince said.

"I'm countin' on you guys."

"No problem, Mr. G.," Bobbo said. "It's in da bag."

As Otash and I left the hospital he said, "Never thought I'd be throwing in with Johnny Roselli."

"Actually," I said, "he's kind of throwin' in with us."

"Even stranger," he said, "only . . ."

"Only what?"

"How can you be sure you can trust these guys?" he asked. "I mean, how do we know they were really sent by Roselli?"

"They mentioned Jack Entratter," I said. "Nobody knows that Jack was callin' Johnny. My only worry is what happens if the cops come back."

"You know, at one time the L.A. Police Department was the most corrupt in the country—even worse than Chicago. There's no reason to believe some of that's not still true."

"You're sayin' they're on Roselli's pad?"

"Roselli's, the FBI, they're on somebody's."

"I kinda thought Stanze was different."

"He may well be," Otash said, "but he's only one man, and he can't buck the whole system."

Sixty-one

WE WENT FROM THE HOSPITAL to Fred Otash's office. It was the beginning of business hours and Miss Deeds was at her desk. He told me he had a private bath off his office, which included a shower. I told him I'd wait until I got back to Marilyn's for the clothes, but I did wash up.

When I came out of the bathroom reasonably refreshed, Otash was sitting at his desk, just hanging up the phone.

"This is no surprise," he said. "The car driven by Harris is registered to the JEH Group."

"We get an address?"

"A PO box."

"What about a driver's license?"

"That's a good thought," Otash said. "You'll make a detective yet. I just checked with my contact in Motor Vehicle. There are too many drivers named Harris for us to tell anything."

"So we go on stakeout?" I asked.

"Yes, with one change," he said.

"What's that?"

"We follow whoever comes out," he said. "Harris, the guy with the scar, or the manager, the other guy whose voice you heard."

"I don't know what he looks like."

"We'll find out," Otash said. "If he's running the place for the FBI he's got to know something."

"What about the bouncer? I heard him say he's running girls out of there."

"Good idea," Otash said. "If he thinks he's going to be pinched for running a string of girls, maybe he'll talk."

"He looks like he'd be used for heavy lifting."

"You mean like moving Danny from the basement to somewhere else?"

"That's what I mean."

I didn't like thinking of Danny as deadweight—or as dead. I wasn't sure how I'd react if I found my longtime friend dead. I just had to keep thinking of him as alive, somewhere.

Penny would never forgive me if I didn't bring him back.

Otash wanted to make some more calls—and use his shower— so instead of hanging around the office and—for some reason I still couldn't figure out—annoying Miss Deeds, I decided to go back to Marilyn's and get my own clothes.

"Be back here in a couple of hours," Otash said. "With any luck I'll know something about the manager and the bouncer at the Lavender."

"Okay," I said. "I'll see you then."

I drove back to the guesthouse, went inside, took a shower and brewed a pot of coffee to try to keep myself awake.

I was standing at the sink, drinking my second cup, when I

saw movement out of the corner of my eye. I froze, kept looking out the window and saw it again. Somebody was moving around inside the main house.

"Goddamnit!" I said angrily. It wasn't bad enough they had sent Jerry to the hospital, they had to come back? And for what?

I went out to my car, opened the trunk as quietly as I could and took out Jerry's .45. Clutching it, I moved around behind the main house to the kitchen. Everybody seemed to be using that door to get in. I was no different. It wasn't locked, so I opened it and slipped inside. At that point someone chose to enter the room. I raised the gun and pointed before I realized it was Marilyn Monroe.

"Jesus Christ!"

Marilyn screamed and jumped back, eyes wide, then recognized me.

"Eddie! You scared the hell out of me!"

"Marilyn, what the hell are you doin' here? I told you to stay at Frank's."

"Frank got real busy with the construction," she said. "I started to feel like I was in the way. I wanted to come home, so he had one of his bodyguards drive me. What are you doing with that gun?"

"It's Jerry's," I said. "He's in the hospital."

"Wha—why? What happened?"

"Look," I said, taking her arm, "let's go in the guesthouse. I just made some coffee. We can talk there."

"But why not here?" she asked, as she trotted to the door.

"This is where Jerry got hurt," I said, "and I'm not sure the people who hurt him won't come back."

She turned to look back at the kitchen as I gently shoved her out the door.

Sixty-two

SEATED AT THE KITCHEN TABLE, with coffee in front of both of us, I told her what had happened to Jerry and where he was.

"My God, Eddie, will he be all right?"

"I hope so."

"You have to make sure the hospital bills get sent to me."

"Dean is already takin' care of it."

"You're here because of me, Eddie," she said. "There's no reason why Dean should pay the bill."

"You'll have to take that up with Dean yourself, Marilyn. Right now I'm not very concerned with hospital bills."

"I know," she said, reaching out and touching my arm, "you're worried about both your friends now."

"I'm worried about all of us, Marilyn," I admitted.

"I'm sorry I came back, Eddie, but I had to. I couldn't stay at Frank's anymore."

"We'll have to find someplace else to stash you," I said.

Her lovely shoulders slumped. "Maybe I should just get used to being watched all the time," she said.

"Watched on the screen, yeah," I said, "or on the red carpet, sure, but not every day, morning, noon and night. Nobody should be watched that much."

"Eddie," she said, "can I sleep with you tonight?"

The question shocked me.

"What?"

"Jerry's in the hospital, so you're out here alone and I'd be in the house alone," she said. "I'm awfully lonely, Eddie."

"Marilyn," I said, "if we do that we might be lookin' for trouble."

"I'm not talking about sex, Eddie," she said. "I just mean . . . sleep next to you. Just so I'm not so alone."

She still had her hand on mine and she squeezed.

"We'll see," I said, squeezing her back. "When tonight comes, we'll see."

She released my hand and sat back in her chair, looking at me. "I'm glad I came back, Eddie," she said. "Real glad."

"When do you have to go to work?" I asked.

She brushed her hair out of her eyes.

"Probably should've been there by now. I'd have to check my schedule with my agent, but you know what? This is the longest I've been in blue jeans and my comfy sweatshirt in a long time. I like it. I think they agree with me."

"It all agrees with you," I said. "You look beautiful."

She took her face in both hands. "I must look awful. My hair, my face."

"You shine, Marilyn," I said, "with or without makeup."

She got a funny look on her face. "Did you see *The Misfits*?"

"No," I said, "I never had the chance. I'm sorry."

"Don't be, only . . . what you just said, it was like a line Clark said to me in the movie. Not word, for word, but he said 'Roslyn, you shine.' . . ."

"I'm sorry if I brought back a bad memory."

"There was a lot about that shoot that was bad," she said,

"but some of it was good. Arthur and me, we were like cats and dogs. That was near the end. But Clark . . . I loved him."

"Were you *in* love with him?"

"Oh, no, I don't mean like that," she said. "He was so in love with Kay, and she was pregnant. No, I just . . . I just meant . . ."

"What?" I asked. "What were you gonna say?"

"Well, I always wanted Clark Gable to be my . . . my father," she said, staring off into space. "Even before I met him. I had this fantasy that he'd adopt me and hug me, bounce me on his knee. That maybe I'd become part of a family." She looked at me and focused again. "Isn't that the most ridiculous thing you've ever heard?"

"No, it isn't," I said. "I mean, as long as you know he's not your father, you know? And that it's just . . . a fantasy."

"Well, of course," she said. "Of course I know that. I'm not crazy."

"I know that, Marilyn," I said. "The rest of the world is crazy, but not you and me."

"No," she said, reaching for my hand again, "not you and me."

Speaking of crazy, I thought . . .

"You know, Marilyn, I'm part of a big Italian family. I have a brother, a sister, and about thirty-two cousins."

"That must be wonderful."

"Well, it's not," I said. "You see, my father is crazy, always has been, and my brother and sister grew up wanting his approval, so they're crazy, too."

"And your mother?"

"She wasn't so much crazy as she was dominated by my old man," I said. "Whenever he'd try to play with my head, or decide to give me a beating, she'd just watch and shrug helplessly."

"That's awful."

"Yes, it is," I said.

"But . . . you said she just died. Were you . . . upset?"

"I was," I said, "but when I went back to Brooklyn for the funeral my father started right in again, and you know what? I got mad at my mother all over again. I was mad at myself for being sucked in again. I never should've gone to the funeral. But Jerry went with me, and saw what happened, and he understood. He's more of a brother than my brother ever was."

"Oh, Eddie." Her eyes got moist and she threw her arms around me. "I guess it's better to have good friends."

"Definitely," I said, "definitely better to have good friends." I squeezed her tightly.

"I've got to go out," I said, releasing her. "Fred Otash is waiting for me."

"Is it about Danny? And Jerry?"

"Yes," I said, "but I've got to put you someplace safe. I better call Fred."

"Don't do that, Eddie. Just leave me here," she said, "in the guesthouse. With no car outside, nobody will know I'm here."

"Marilyn, I don't think that's a good idea."

"Just for today," she said. "You have things to do and I've surprised you. Go and do what you've got to do. I promise I'll stay out of sight."

I hesitated and she knew she had me.

"Go on, your private eye is waiting for you."

"Okay," I said, "but remember, stay inside. I think there's some food in the fridge, thanks to Jerry."

"Good," she said, standing up. "I'll have something to eat later."

I stood and she took my arm, walked me to the back door.

"Be careful, Eddie," she said. "I'll be waiting here when you're done."

"Okay, now move away from the door."

"You think someone's watching us right now?"

"I hope not," I said, "but just to be safe."

"All right," she said, backing away, her hands behind her back. "There, now you can leave. I'll see you later."

"I'll try not to be away too long, but if somethin' happens I'll call."

I went out the door, hoping I wasn't making a big mistake. Otash and I were on the verge of finding Danny—at least, that's what I was tellin' myself—and she *had* surprised me by showing up. To change my plans now might mean never finding Danny.

I just wished she had stayed at Frank's.

When I got to the car I opened the door to get in. "Close it back up, Eddie."

I turned and saw two men. One was Harris, and the one holding a revolver had a livid scar almost dead center down his forehead.

"We thought it was time we got acquainted, Eddie," the man with the scar said, "seein' as how you're bein' such a pain in the ass."

Sixty-three

PAIN IN THE ASS?" I asked. "Me? I don't even know you guys."

"Start walkin'," Harris said.

We headed back to the house with me in the lead.

"Not the big one," the man with the scar said.

Damn it. I was hoping to lead them away from Marilyn.

"Yeah, you've been a pain," the scarred man said. "Because of you we had to kill that Johnson guy."

"Why?" I asked. "He lied when I came back with the cops. And he wiped the records clean."

"He would've talked eventually," Harris said. "Nope, we agreed he had to go."

"And your buddy, Bardini—" the scarred man started.

"Did you kill him, too?" I asked, cutting him off. "Or is he alive somewhere?"

"And you were seen in the club," Harris said, "you and your private eye."

"Only we can't kill him," the scarred man said. "He's got too high a profile—or so we're told."

"Told by who?" I asked. "The FBI?"

The two men looked at each other.

"Boy," Harris said, "any chance you had of walkin' away from this just went out the window."

Me and my big mouth.

I thought about making them kill me right there and then, so that they wouldn't go any farther and find Marilyn. Maybe I wasn't brave enough to do it, or maybe I was just holding onto my life as long as I could, figuring that something would happen to save me.

I headed for the front door of the guesthouse, but once again they directed me.

"Back door, sport," Harris said.

"What were you doin' in the house yesterday?" I asked. "Why'd you hit Jerry?"

"What are you talkin' about?" Harris asked, his eyes going all jerky.

"Who's Jerry?" the scarred man asked. "That your big buddy?"

"Come on," I said, "you laid him out and put him in the hospital by ambushing him."

The scarred man looked at his partner and asked, "What's he talkin' about, Harris?"

"Nothin'," Harris said. "He's just tryin' to save his ass."

We reached the back door.

"You got a key?" Harris asked.

"Of course."

"Maybe it's open," Harris said, reaching for the door.

"No," I said, pushing past him, "I locked it. I'll use the key."

The door was unlocked, but I jiggled the doorknob like I was using the key, hoping Marilyn would hear us and hide.

"Hold it," Harris said, as I pushed the door open. "I'm goin' first."

I backed away. "Be my guest."

He walked in ahead of me and suddenly there was a scream and a sound, like metal on bone. Harris went down like he'd been poleaxed.

I didn't wait, I reacted and backed into the scarred man, who stood startled by what had just happened to his partner. We got tangled up, stumbled back together and fell to the ground. I tried to grab his gun hand, but he managed to roll away from me. He got to his feet with his back to the house. I was on the ground on my back. He pointed the gun down at me and I waited for the sound of the shot, or the muzzle flash. Suddenly Marilyn came flying out of the house with a cast-iron frying pan in her hand.

"Leave him alone!" she screamed, and swung the frying pan.

The man turned at the sound of her voice and the frying pan caught him right on the forehead. I saw blood fly and he went down, the gun dropping from his hand.

"Eddie—" Marilyn said.

"Bitch!" Harris shouted, staggering out of the house. His face was covered with blood and he was trying to clear it from his eyes so he could use the gun in his hand.

I scrambled on all fours, grabbed up scar face's gun from the ground and turned it on Harris. He was still blind, but if he decided to start squeezing off shots Marilyn might get hit. I pointed the revolver at him and pulled the trigger three times. All three shots hit him and drove him back through the doorway and into the house.

I got to my feet and Marilyn came running over to me.

"Are you all right, Eddie?"

"Yeah, I am, thanks to you."

I hugged her tightly. "Are you all right?" I asked.

"Yes," she said, "I heard you at the door, and the voices. I looked out the window over the sink and saw that man with the gun. I didn't know what to do, so I grabbed a frying pan and hit the first guy through the door."

"I'm glad it wasn't me."

"Are they dead?"

"I'm gonna check," I said. "Just stand here a minute."

I checked the one on the ground first. Marilyn's frying pan had split his head right along that old scar line. He was deader than dead.

I went into the guesthouse and leaned over Harris. He was dead.

"Damn it!" I shouted.

"Eddie? What's wrong?" Marilyn stuck her head in the door.

"They're both dead," I said, "now we can't find out what they did with Danny."

"Oh." She looked like a scolded little girl.

"Hey, hey," I said, taking the pan from her and setting it aside, "I'm not mad at you. You did the right thing. Marilyn, you saved our lives."

"I did?" she asked, and then nodded and said, "I did."

"Why don't you go and sit in the living room?" I asked. "I'm gonna call the cops, and Otash."

"Okay, Eddie."

She went into the other room and I wondered how long it was going to take for it to dawn on her that she had killed a man.

Sixty-four

HALF AN HOUR LATER Marilyn was sitting in the living room of the guesthouse, perched on the edge of the sofa, hugging herself tightly. She didn't realize that the position was pushing her breasts up out of her sweatshirt so that there was a lot of pale cleavage for the cops and technicians to stare at.

I called Detective Stanze over to one side and said, "Do you think we could get your men to stop drooling over Marilyn's tits for five minutes?"

"Come on, Eddie," he said, "it's Marilyn Monroe, for chrissake. You don't want them looking then get her to cover up."

"Can I move her to the main house?"

"No," he said, "this is where everything happened, and I want her here."

He was pissed at me for calling him to the scene with two dead men on the ground. Or maybe it was because the FBI had gotten him yanked from the case, and here he was back in it again.

"Let me through!" I heard Fred Otash shout from the kitchen.

Stanze heard it, too, and he craned his neck and said, "Let him in."

Moments later Otash came stalking into the living room.

"What the hell happened?" he demanded, looking at me. "I thought you told me she was out of town."

"She was," I said, "I didn't expect her back here."

"And these two just happened to pick today to take you out of the picture?" Otash asked.

"Yeah," I said. "They said they killed the desk clerk, and grabbed Danny, and now I was a big enough pain in the neck that they had to kill me, too."

"So they killed Danny?" Otash asked.

"I don't know," I said. "I couldn't get a firm answer out of them and then . . . they were dead."

"No, not 'and then they were dead,'" Stanze said. "You killed them."

"So they wouldn't kill us."

"What I want to know is how you killed one with a frying pan and one with a gun?"

"I told you already."

"Yes, I know," Stanze said, "but it doesn't sound logical to me."

"None of this has seemed logical to me," I said, "especially the part where you pulled your men from the hospital."

"I told you that wasn't my decision, but I have to follow orders."

"No matter who they come from."

"They came from my boss!"

"And where did his orders come from?" I demanded.

"Ah!" Stanze said, and stormed off into the kitchen.

"How the hell are we going to find out what happened to Danny now?" I asked.

"There's only one place we can get answers from," Otash said.

"Where?"

"The FBI. The problem is, how to get the FBI to talk to us?"

"I don't know," I said as a thought hit me, "I might have to make a few calls."

"To who?"

"Tell you later, but I've got another question for you."

"What's that?"

"These guys claimed they didn't know anything about Jerry gettin' clobbered," I said.

"Well, if that's true, then who slugged Jerry, and why?"

"Those are the questions."

Sixty-five

STANZE FINALLY LET ME take Marilyn back to the main house.

"Eddie," she said, when we got inside, "it's going to be in the newspapers that I killed a guy."

"No," I said, "it's gonna be in the paper that I killed two men in your guesthouse . . . in self-defense."

"B-but, you can't take the blame for something I did," she said.

"Sure I can," I said. "Nobody cares about me. This will all be in the papers because it's your house, but it'll soon become old news. The other way, if we tell them you killed one, it'll be in the news forever."

"But I'll always know," she said. "It was terrible. I can still hear the sound and see all that blood—"

"Marilyn, those guys were gonna kill me," I said, "and if they found you in the house, they might've killed you, too. I told you before. You saved our lives."

"Okay," she said, "okay, Eddie. I think I'm going to go to my room and lie down."

"That's a good idea."

As she left the room somebody knocked on the front door. I went and let Otash in.

"How is she?"

"Shaken up," I said. "She went to lay down."

"You're taking a chance, you know, taking all the blame," he said.

"I don't think so," I said. "Looks pretty cut-and-dried to me. They were gonna kill me, for sure, and who knows what they would've done to her if they'd found her there."

"I agree."

"You can feel pretty safe though," I said.

"How's that?"

"They said you were too high-profile to kill."

"I'll try not to let that go to my head. So, let's see where we stand now?"

"I killed the only two men who might've told us what they did with Danny, that's where we stand—officially."

"There's still the Lavender and the guy who manages it," Otash said. "We could sweat him."

"I don't think we have time for that, Fred. After all this if Danny's still alive they might decide to get rid of him."

"So what do you suggest?"

"I've got a phone number," I said. "I don't know if it's still good, but I can try it."

"And who would be at the other end of that number?"

"Well," I said, "last year it was Joseph Kennedy, but I actually got a call back from JFK."

"The president?"

"That's the only JFK I know of," I said.

"And these are the sort of contacts you make as a pit boss in Vegas? Who else, besides show business people and politicians?"

"Those are pretty much my specialty."

I took out my wallet and extracted a slip of paper with a phone number on it that had been there for months.

Otash lowered his voice and asked, "You sure you want to make that call from here?"

He was referring to the fact that I felt sure the house was bugged.

"Oh, yes," I said, "I want everybody involved to know about this phone call."

I dialed and was pleased to hear it ring. I waited for someone to answer.

Otash and I played gin for more than two hours before the phone rang.

I had just checked on Marilyn, found her asleep in her bed, lying atop the comforter. Next to her, on the night table, were some pill bottles, all with the caps on tight. I looked at the labels, recognized a couple that were for sleeping, and then I saw Nembutal and chloral hydrate. There was no water or any liquid on the table, no glass, but she could have gone into the bathroom and taken them there. The bottles, however, all had a healthy amount of pills inside.

At that moment she opened her eyes and smiled when she saw me. Her eyes were sleepy, but clear. "Is everything all right, Eddie?"

"Sure, kid, everything's fine," I said. "Go back to sleep."

She closed her eyes and seemed to fall back to sleep in seconds. I had the feeling she was exhausted, and that being home was going to be good for her after all.

I leaned in close to her. She smelled wonderful and I could see the pulse beneath the pale flesh of her throat beating strongly. Everything I saw led me to believe she was sleeping peacefully.

"How is she?" Otash asked when I came out.

"Sleeping," I said. "She's got a lot of pills on her night table, but I don't think she took any."

"She breathing okay?"

"Fine," I said.

"I mean, I've heard stories—"

"She's fine, Fred."

I didn't bother telling him what pills were on her table, but I vowed to look into it myself later on.

So we went on playing gin after I checked on Marilyn and when the phone rang we both jumped.

"Jesus," he said.

We stared at the phone as it rang a second time.

"That could be the president," he said.

"Could be."

"Of the United States."

I snatched it up so it wouldn't ring a third time and maybe wake Marilyn.

"Hello?"

"Eddie?"

"That's right." I recognized the broad Massachusetts accent.

"Eddie, I know you wanted to speak to Jack, but he's unavailable. Will I do?"

"Yes, sir," I said, realizing I was talking to Bobby, "the attorney general will do just fine."

Sixty-six

I LAID IT OUT for the attorney general of the United States and he listened quietly.

"I think I am most surprised by Marilyn's reaction," Bobby Kennedy said when I finished.

"Not quite the delicate flower everyone thinks she is," I said, "at least not with a frying pan in her hand."

I told him about the whole ordeal, but not that she had killed the man. I still maintained I had killed them both.

"Eddie, I think you should give me a little time, and then go over to the Lavender Club to find your friend."

"What about the FBI?" I asked.

"It seems you've taken care of their freelancers," RFK said, "but, Eddie, I really think you should leave Edgar to me." It sounded like he said "Edgah."

"I think I know what you're tellin' me, sir."

"Let me make it clear," RFK said. "I'm telling you to be satisfied to get your friend back. Be satisfied that Jerry is alive. And be satisfied that you've taken care of the two freelancers who, in all probability, were watching Marilyn. And I don't think there will be any charges brought against you."

"So I just let it go that the FBI was behind the whole thing?"

"As I said," Kennedy repeated, "Edgar must be left to me. I'm used to dealing with him."

"And what do I tell Marilyn?"

"That she won't be bothered anymore."

"Is that true?"

He hesitated, then said, "It's the best thing you can tell her."

I fell silent. I wasn't sure I was comfortable with what he was telling me.

"Eddie?"

"Yes, sir."

"Believe me, this is the best way," he said. "Let me make some calls, and then you go over to the Lavender Club—which will probably be padlocked by tomorrow."

"Yes, sir."

"My father and brother tell me you're a reasonable man."

"I have been."

"Well then, continue to be," Kennedy said, "and everything will go your way."

"My friend, Danny, has to be alive, sir, for me to be reasonable in even the smallest way."

"Just give me some time and then you can go pick him up."

"Yes, sir."

I hung up and stared at Otash.

"Bobby Kennedy?" he asked.

"He says we can go and pick up Danny in a little while."

"Where?"

"The Lavender Club, which he says will be closed down by tomorrow."

"And?"

"And then everything is over."

"And the FBI's involvement?"

"The attorney general asked me to leave them to him. He says he's used to dealing with Hoover."

"That's all over my head," Otash said. "You'd better go along, Eddie."

"Yeah, I know," I said, "it's always better just to go along, isn't it?"

Sixty-seven

THE BOUNCER STOPPED US at the door.

"By invitation only tonight, gents," he said. "It's our last night."

Well, if I was wondering if Robert Kennedy had made his phone calls, that clinched it.

"We have invitations," I said.

"Let's see 'em."

"Tell your boss Eddie G is here."

The bouncer smiled. "Eddie G. That's it?"

"Believe me, that'll be enough."

The bouncer stopped frowning and took a second look at Otash, standing next to me. "Hey, I know you."

"Not officially," Otash said.

"What's your na—"

"Eddie G is all you need," I said. "Now hurry. We're all on a tight schedule."

The man wanted to argue, but obviously wasn't sure of his footing. "Wait here."

He went into the building, locking the door behind him. It took ten minutes for him to return.

"Come on."

We followed him inside. For a private party it was remarkably well attended. It looked like standing room only and apparently all the girls were on the runways. The music was too loud to think or speak, so he just beckoned us to follow him.

Down the hall again, this time with permission, and into the office. The man behind the desk looked up and frowned at me. His hair was painfully red and if he had smiled he would have looked like he belonged on the cover of *Mad* magazine. The Hawaiian shirt he was wearing was even more painful than his hair.

But he didn't smile at me.

"Are you the guy who left the light on in the basement?" he asked.

"That was me," I said.

"I'm gonna send you my electric bill."

"What, the FBI won't pay it?"

"And you're also the reason I'm being shut down?" he demanded.

"Probably."

The man covered his face.

"I'm gonna have to start wearing a suit again."

"I guess you should've snatched somebody else's friend."

"Is that what this is all about?" he asked, waving his hand. "He's fine."

"Unlike Max Johnson."

"Who? Oh, yeah, the hotel clerk. That was those two idiot freelancers, Harris and Delaney. I understand you killed them?"

"They needed it," Otash said, butting in. Maybe he was feeling left out. "The FBI must be falling on hard times to employ those two."

"When you employ for the purpose of deniability there's no point in making it top talent, is there?"

"So if I hadn't killed them—"

"Somebody would've."

"Wait a minute," Otash said, "you're actually an FBI agent?"

"Born and bred," the man said. "Twenty years, right out of college. My father was an agent before me, but he never had a sweet gig like this."

"And him?" Otash asked, jerking his thumb at the bouncer.

"Just a bouncer," the man said.

"And a pimp," I said.

"What?" The agent looked surprised.

"Hey," the bouncer said.

"Last time I was here I heard him saying he ran a string of girls out of here."

The agent looked at the bouncer.

"Peter, I'm very disappointed in you," he said. "Damn it. Now I'm gonna have to arrest you."

"Damn it, Sam, I was just—"

Sam (Kearny, no doubt), the FBI agent, took a gun out of his top drawer and shot Peter the bouncer. Peter looked shocked, grabbed his stomach and fell facedown on the floor.

Otash and I didn't move. I think we both realized we were in the hands of a crazy man.

Kearny put the gun back in his top drawer.

"There," he said, "I'm back on the right side of the law, aren't I?"

"How long have you been under?" Otash asked.

"Would've been five years next week," Kearny said. "I had a helluva celebration planned. Now next week I'll be back in an office in Washington."

"Um . . . I'm sorry?" I said.

He waved my apology away. "Don't be. It had to end some

time." He stood up, straightened his Hawaiian shirt. "All right, come with me."

He walked past us, out the door. We followed him down the hall to the basement door.

"You've been here before," he said to me, "so mind your step."

We went down the steps and he pulled on a new string someone had attached to the bulb, which was now a forty watt white.

The man seated in the wooden chair looked up at us. He had a lopsided grin on a bruised face.

"Damn it," Danny said, "what took you so long, Eddie?"

Amazingly, the crazy fed let us all go.

"I'd invite you to stay for the party, but I'm actually pretty pissed at you," he said at the front door. "Hope I don't run into you again."

"Likewise," I said, as the door closed.

Now that we were outside I grabbed Danny in a bear hug.

"Goddamnit, man, I was starting to think that you were dead."

"Lemme go, I got sore ribs!" he said, pushing me away. "They knocked me around a bit, but never really came close to killing me. How's Penny doin'?"

"Worried sick."

"And Marilyn?"

"I'll tell you in the car," I said, and then, "Oh, yeah, meet Fred Otash. Fred, Danny Bardini."

"Hey, I know you," Danny said, as they shook hands. "I saw your ad. How much did that set you back?"

"Like Eddie said, I'll tell you in the car."

We walked to my Caddy.

"You want to go to the hospital?" I asked.

"Naw, you know what I really want?" he asked. "A burger and a beer."

I looked at Otash.

"I'm kinda hungry myself."

"Okay," I said, "but let's go pick up Marilyn and we'll make it a foursome."

"I get to meet her?" Danny asked happily. His smile was so wide it split a scab on his lip.

"After what you've been through, old buddy," I said, "it's the least I can do. But first you've got to call Penny."

Sixty-eight

A COUPLE OF DAYS later I drove to Palm Springs with two passengers, Danny and Jerry. Jerry had awakened the day before in his room with the two Johnny Roselli men watching him, took one look at them and said, "Hi, guys."

Once he was awake there was no keeping him in the hospital. He was upset that I had gotten into a shoot-out without him, and he wanted to be by my side in case the FBI came after me.

Marilyn wanted Jerry to stay with her in the main house so she could baby him, and as appealing as that sounded, the big guy turned her down. We did continue to stay in her guesthouse, but that was it.

"Ya can't trust the feds, Mr. G.," he said, "and as long as I'm awake, I'm with ya."

Taking Danny to Frank's was the least I could do for him. Also, he wanted to go back to the motel, but I put him in a hotel not too far from Marilyn's, that had room service and a pool.

So we pulled up to Frank's place with a bandaged Jerry in the front seat and a bruised Danny in the back. I felt guilty that they had taken the brunt of the punishment.

"This is great, Eddie," he said, looking at Frank's Palm Spring enclave.

I stopped the car and turned off the engine. I could hear raised voices as George came down the stairs toward us.

"What's goin' on, George?" I asked.

"This is not a good day to visit, Mr. Gianelli."

"Why not?"

"Mr. S. has gotten some bad news today."

"From who?" Danny asked.

"Oh, George, this is my friend Danny, the one I've been lookin' for."

"Ah, so glad to see you looking so . . . well, sir."

"Yeah, a few bruises, one cracked rib . . . but thanks. So what gives?"

George looked at Jerry. "Are *you* all right, sir?"

"I'm fine, George, thanks."

"Mr. Lawford came to see Mr. S. today," George said, leading the way up the stairs. "I'm afraid he told him that the president would not be staying here, as planned."

"Oh," I said. "That *is* bad news."

When we reached the top we could see Frank and Peter Lawford on the newly constructed wing. Frank was doing all the shouting, with Peter throwing in a plea or two when he could.

"Goddamn useless limey sonofa—" Frank was shouting.

"Not my fault, Frank," was all we heard from Peter, and then suddenly he was tumbling backward down the stairs from the second level. I had never liked him, but I felt sorry for him, caught between the Kennedys and Frank.

As Peter hit the ground Frank came running down the steps. He stepped over Peter, walked around the side of the building and came back holding a sledgehammer.

"Is he gonna—" Danny said.

"I hope not."

Peter was moving, which meant he wasn't dead. But if Frank

took the sledgehammer to him, that could change. Frank stalked over to the concrete helipad he'd had constructed for JFK and began wailing away at it with the hammer. For a skinny guy, he was putting a lot of power behind it, and the concrete began to crumble.

"Ya want I should help Mr. S., Mr. G.?"

"No, Jerry," I said. "Swingin' a sledgehammer would only put you back in the hospital. Besides, I think Frank needs to do this himself."

"He's that mad about JFK not comin'?" Danny asked. "Maybe he'll visit another time."

"It's not just that," George said. "Mr. Lawford told Frank that the president would be staying at Bing Crosby's house."

"Whoa," I said.

"Maybe we'd better—" Danny said.

"Yeah," I said, "we better. George, you go help Peter up and get him out of here. Tell Frank we'll stop by another time."

"Yes, sir," George said. "Sorry, sir."

"That's okay, George," I said. "We understand."

As we headed back to the Caddy we could hear Frank grunting with every swing of the sledgehammer, and in between every grunt, the cursing.

"Where are we headed now?" Danny asked.

"I've got one more favor to do for Marilyn."

"Where?"

"Encino."

"Clark Gable's," Jerry told Danny.

Clark Gable's house was not a house, it was a ranch.

"Jesus," Danny said, as we drove the winding drive. "What are you gonna say to make her see you?"

"I don't know," I said. "We'll just try knocking on the door and see what happens."

Jerry liked the horses we saw cantering in the pastures.

"The only horses I ever see in New York has got cops on 'em."

We drove up to the front of the house and parked. There were no other cars in view, but there could have been a dozen of them out of sight.

Walking up to the door Danny asked, "Got a story, yet?"

"I think I'll just tell her the truth."

We stopped at the door and I knocked. I expected it to be opened by a butler, or some kind of servant, but it was opened by an attractive, dark-haired woman.

"Yes? Oh, my. You poor men. What happened?" she said to Danny.

The bruises on his face had faded, but were still there. His lip stayed split because he kept smiling like a love-struck kid around Marilyn Monroe. Jerry still had a bandage covering his entire head.

"Oh," Danny said, "a car accident. But I'm okay."

"Yes, ma'am," Jerry said, "me, too."

"Well, then what can I do for you gentlemen?" she asked.

"Mrs. Gable," I said, "my name is Eddie Gianelli. I'm a friend of Marilyn Monroe's. May I speak with you, please?"

"Marilyn?" she asked. "How is she?"

"Well," I said, "I guess that's going to depend on you."

Sixty-nine

WE SPENT ONE MORE NIGHT at Marilyn's, three guys who, three weeks ago, thought of her only as a sex symbol. Now, Marilyn's vulnerability had turned her into someone we adored and wanted to protect.

That night, while Jerry and Danny argued over the TV like a couple of brothers, I sat in the kitchen with Marilyn.

"I talked to Kay Gable yesterday," I said. I'd kept it from her until that moment.

"Oh, God, Eddie, what did she say?"

"Marilyn, you didn't tell me that Kay invited you to the baby's christening last year."

"Oh, yeah," she said, "I forgot about that."

"And you went?"

"Yes."

"How did she treat you?"

"She treated me fine, Eddie," she said, her eyes lowered.

"Then what are you worried about?"

"Well . . . that was in front of people. She could've invited me, you know, so she'd look . . . oh, Eddie, I want to know what she thinks inside."

"She thinks Gable exerted himself unnecessarily in a hot desert for the length of the shoot. She thinks he went on a dangerous crash diet, lost too much weight too fast, put a strain on his heart, and died. Gable was fifty-nine, Marilyn."

She looked down again and her shoulders slumped. "I know all that, Eddie."

"Remember what we said about good friends, Marilyn?" I asked.

"Yes."

"You have to learn to rely on your good friends more. And as far as I can see, Kay Gable is a good friend."

"Really, Eddie?"

"Really. Marilyn, you've got to stop worrying about what people think. You need to go back to work."

"I know," she said. "They're trying to kick me off this picture, replace me with Lee Remick, but Dean is fighting to keep me on."

"Dean's another good friend."

She reached out and grabbed my hands.

"Right now you're my best friend, Eddie."

"I'm one of your friends, doll, and you're one of mine. What a pair we make."

I brought her hands to my lips and kissed them.

"I love you, Eddie."

"I love you, too, kid."

Epilogue

THAT WAS . . . FASCINATING, Eddie," J.T. Kerouac said. "But who hit Jerry?"

"You know, we never found out," I said. "I think either Harris or Delaney did it, and didn't want the other one to know they were prowling around Marilyn's house. There was a point there, when they had the gun on me, where they looked confused and nervous. My money's on Harris."

"So then you killing them must've made Jerry real happy."

In the telling of the story to J.T. I had changed a few things. I told her the same version I told Stanze, that I had killed the two men.

"Actually, no. Jerry said he was sorry I had to kill them. He knew it was something he could've forgotten, but I couldn't."

"What's Jerry doing now?" she asked.

"That's not part of the story."

"Well, how much of this can I use?"

"Use? None of it."

"What?"

"It was all off-the-record. I mean, use anything I said about old Vegas, or the Rat Pack, but nothing I told you about Marilyn is for public use."

"But . . . you told me the story. I've got it all down on tape," she said, touching the mini-recorder on the table.

"The meanderings of an old man," I said. It wasn't far from the truth. I tended to go on when people would let me talk about old Vegas.

"Eddie . . . why?"

"Because I don't want anything I say to alter Marilyn's legend?"

"Legend? She was a pathetic woman who couldn't have a lasting relationship. Her only success was what she was in the imaginations of men."

"That's the slant you'll be takin'?" I asked.

"What else is there?"

"She was much more than you think, much more than most people think."

Maybe I should have told her that Marilyn saved both our lives, but I knew if I did that the newspapers the next day would all carry the same headline: MARILYN MONROE COMMITTED MURDER.

"Take a walk with me," I said.

"Where?"

"Just a stroll through the casino. Come on."

"I need to bring my recorder, my notes—"

"No, this really is off the record. Leave them there," I said, "I'll tell Melina to watch 'em. Nobody's gonna touch 'em."

"Well, okay . . ."

We got up and I conferred briefly with Melina, who nodded. We left the coffee shop by the door that took us directly into the casino. I exchanged greetings with several waitress and dealers, as well as a casino host. We didn't have casino hosts back during the Rat Pack days. If we had, maybe I never would've met the guys because some host would have been put in charge of seeing to their needs.

"You're still known by a lot of people, Eddie," J.T. said.

"Everybody in this town wants to stay connected to old Vegas," I said. "But all around us are the signs of new Vegas. Look, right there."

I pointed to a slot machine that had Dean Martin's voice singing, "How lucky can one man be, I kissed her and she kissed me . . ."

"Dean Martin slot machines," I said. "Dino must be turnin' over in his grave. Look, over there . . . Elvis machines . . . Frank Sinatra machines . . . and come over here with me."

I led J.T. to a bank of machines against a wall. There were four of them, the new kind, like TV sets rather than upright slot machines.

Above each machine was a different photo of Marilyn, and in each she was smiling and wearing a different gown.

"I don't approve of all these things," I said to J.T., "but they prove one thing. These people are all icons, especially Marilyn."

"Eddie, there are a lot of icons, that doesn't mean they were good people."

"Well, Marilyn was good people," I said. "If you write that I'll swear to it."

One of the shots above the slot machines was the one from *The Seven Year Itch*, with her standing in that white dress over the street grate. Back in the 1960s I never suspected how slot machines would grow and take over as the biggest moneymakers in Vegas. And I certainly never expected to see my friends pop up all around me in casino after casino.

"Okay, Eddie," J.T. said, "I won't use it."

"You won't?"

"No," she said, "but tell me, what did you tell Marilyn? I mean, about being followed, and watched."

"I struggled with that," I said. "I really did, but I decided to put her mind at ease. I told her she was safe, that nobody was watching her anymore."

"You lied to her then," she said.

"Yes," I said, "I did."

"How did you feel after her death?"

"I was devastated."

"Do you think she died because you lied to her?"

I turned and looked at her. "Why, J.T.," I said, "I think you're turnin' mean."

"I'm just tryin' to get my story, Mr. Gianelli," she said, and stormed off.

"Eddie?"

Melina was coming toward me. She handed me J.T. Kerouac's tape. "I took another tape from her bag and replaced it."

"Thanks, Melina. You're a doll."

"Anything for you, Eddie."

"Here," I said, handing her a twenty, "I know she's gonna stiff you on your tip."

"Thanks."

I wondered how J.T. would feel when she got to her booth and found her notes gone.

I sat for a moment in front of one of the Marilyn machines. The night she died she had called Peter Lawford. He was supposed to have been the last person she spoke to. But that wasn't true.

She had called me . . .

Las Vegas, Nevada
August 5, 1962
4:04 A.M.

"Eddie . . ."

"Marilyn?" I was home that morning because it was my night off. I glanced blearily at the clock next to my bed.

"Marilyn, what's wrong?"

"Everything, Eddie," she said, "everything's wrong. It's . . . all over."

"What's all over?" She sounded sleepy . . . or drugged.

"They won't talk to me, Eddie . . . Jack, Bobby . . . I called Peter, but he won't help . . . I talked to Joe . . . but you're the only one who can help me."

I immediately felt guilty. I had only spoken with Marilyn a couple of times over the past seven months. I had returned to Vegas, to my life, and read about her, or heard about her on the news, like everybody else. I called her once, she called me once, but we went back to our own lives.

"Help me, Eddie . . ."

"Marilyn, what did you do?" I asked. "Honey, talk to me. Did you take anything?"

"Pills . . . I have pills, Eddie . . ."

"Yes, but did you take them?"

I remembered the bottles I'd seen at her bedside that day, among them Nembutal and chloral hydrate. I'd meant to talk to her about them, but I never did. After Jerry got out of the hospital we had all said good-bye and driven back to Vegas. Danny returned to work, Jerry flew back to New York and I went back to the Sands.

Apparently, Marilyn had gone back to her private demons.

"Marilyn?"

"Eddie . . . help . . ."

The line went dead.

I dressed and got into my Caddy, drove as fast as I could to

L.A. I drove so fast I was stopped twice by the police, and neither time did they believe that I was rushing to L.A. to try to save Marilyn Monroe. They both gave me speeding tickets.

By the time I arrived at Marilyn's house the police were there, and so was a crowd outside. I saw them remove her body, and I cried, but nobody noticed, because there were plenty of other people crying too . . .

Las Vegas, Nevada
2003

Years later, of course, there are so many different stories about Marilyn's death, but I had seen the Nembutal and chloral hydrate on her night table myself. And one report said they attributed her death to an overdose, even though no glass had ever been found. But I always thought she could have taken the pills in the bathroom and then stumbled back to bed.

But the majority of people in the world don't care about how she died. They only care that she lives on in movies, and in books and, of course, on slot machines.

God help us.

Author's Note

Detective Stanze was named in honor of Police Officer Robert Stanze, a St. Louis policeman who was killed in the line of duty. Deb House, Officer Stanze's sister, emailed to tell me that she and her mother enjoyed my books, and asked if it would be possible to surprise her mother and name a character after him. It was my pleasure to do so. Deb, her mother, and other members of her family—including Officer Stanze's widow—then attended a book signing of mine at Big Sleep Books in St. Louis. It was very gratifying to meet them all and to find out about MOCOPS.

MOCOPS (Missouri Concerns of Police Survivors) is a chapter of the National Concerns of Police Survivors, Inc. (C.O.P.S.). These organizations come to the immediate aide of families of fallen police officers to assist in rebuilding their lives. I'm happy to give a shout-out here to MOCOPS, and commend them on the work they do. Check out their Web site at: www.missouri cops.org.

In 1972, when the actress Veronica Hamel and her husband bought Marilyn's house they brought contractors in to put on a new roof. In removing the old one the contractors discovered all sorts of surveillance equipment that was said to be "standard FBI issue."

The presence of the equipment is odd because one report of the events following Marilyn's death has Fred Otash being sent in to "sweep" the house for bugs and to remove them.

Bibliography

Rat Pack Confidential by Shawn Levy, Doubleday, 1998; The Rat Pack by Lawrence J. Quirk and William Schoell, Taylor Publishing Company, 1998; Dino by Nick Tosches, Dell Publishing, 1992; His Way: The Unauthorized Biography of Frank Sinatra by Kitty Kelley, Bantam Books, 1986; Gonna Do Great Things: The Life of Sammy Davis, Jr. by Gary Fishgall, Scribner, 2003; Sammy Davis Jr.: Me and My Shadow by Arthur Silber Jr., Smart Enterprises, 2002; Sammy: An Autobiography by Sammy Davis Jr. and June and Burt Boyar, Farrar, Straus and Giroux, 2000; Photo by Sammy Davis, Jr., Regan Books, 2007; The Peter Lawford Story: Life with the Kennedys, Monroe and the Rat Pack by Patricia Seaton Lawford, Carroll & Graf Publishers, 1988; Mouse in the Rat Pack: The Joey Bishop Story by Michael Seth Starr, Taylor Trade Publishing, 2002; The Frank Sinatra Film Guide by Daniel O'Brien, BT Batsford, 1998; The Last Good Time: Skinny D'Amato, the Notorious 500 Club, and the Rise and Fall of Atlantic City, by Jonathan Van Meter, Crown Publishers, 2003; Casino: Love and Honor in Las Vegas by Nicholas Pileggi, Simon & Schuster, 1995; Las Vegas Is My Beat by

Ralph Pearl, Bantam Books, 1973, 1974; *Murder in Sin City: The Death of a Las Vegas Casino Boss* by Jeff German, Avon Books, 2001; *A Short History of Reno* by Barbara and Myrick Land, University of Nevada Press, 1995; *A Short History of Las Vegas* by Barbara Land and Myrick Land, University of Nevada Press, 1999, 2004; *When the Mob Ran Vegas* by Steve Fischer, Berkline Press, 2005, 2006; *Mr. S: My Life with Frank Sinatra* by George Jacobs and William Stadiem, HarperCollins, 2003; *Marilyn Monroe* by Donald Spoto, HarperCollins, 1993.